WITHDRAWN

Sundogs and Sunsets

Sundogs and Sunsets

Patricia McNitt Spross

Art by Doug McNitt

Wilderness Adventure Books
1990

Library of Congress Catalog Number 90 — 070253

ISBN: 0 — 923568 — 09 — 3

Cover design by
Doug McNitt

Typesetting by
LaserText Typesetting Services
3886 Sheldrake Avenue
Okemos, Michigan 48864

PUBLISHED BY

Wilderness Adventure Books
320 Garden Lane
Box 968
Fowlerville, Michigan 48836

Manufactured in the United States of America

To Harold

Contents

September

October

Acknowledgement.

Did all of this happen? Of course not in exactly this way. I have made the bad much worse and the good much, much better which is the way of great old yarns.

These are the people of my mind and heart. And to all of them, my thanks for giving me rich memories and a lifetime of unbelievable fun.

There is no Hollandsville, or Cumosette River or Fillson. Us Kids did live on the two Old Farms with all their joys and delights. Mother did tell me the strange, mystical yarns and we did live through years of hardship and poverty without ever realizing it was difficult.

I am grateful to all my family who helped me to remember "how it was then." To Clayton Johnson for answering my many questions about techniques for driving a Model T, hog butchering, cleaning bullheads and many more. And to all who read the manuscript and took time to give me kind criticism and helpful encouragement.

Special thanks are due to Brenda Lockwood who has kept me working when I have been discouraged, listened countless hours to the text, offered generous praise and wise criticism, chased my commas, corrected my English usage and been a good friend through two years of literary procrastination.

And very special thanks to Harold whose laughter and love give me purpose for my existence.

Patricia McNitt Spross
Okemos, Michigan
1990

Early spring days were a special time for Us Kids. Often Father called to us, "Come out and see the sundog!" We had absolutely no idea what caused sundogs, only regarded them as portentous blazing streaks of gold and red on either side of the sun put there for our special pleasure.

While we watched, Father never failed to remark, "It's going to storm." And we agreed, nodding wisely. We were sure he was right. Sundogs told us to get ready for weather.

At the end of day, Father called from the backyard. "Come out and see the sunset." Then we all went out to sit on chunks by the woodpile behind the house to watch the sun go down over the chicken coop roof.

In summer, the night noises came. Insects buzzing, horses stomping in their stalls, the pigs in the Old Shed giving a few last hungry "Snuffle, shruggles" and the chickens' soft, whispering chirps as they fluttered up to the roosts. And all around us, the day folding up for the night to wait for another morning. It was a good time and kept us close.

NO GRILLED CHEESE

Monday, July 13. A few
mornings ago, as I snuggled Grandmother into the seat beside me in the Old Chevy, it occurred to me that all the
seminars on successful retirement never mentioned the fun
it might prove to be. Neither did they prepare me for feel-
ings of being in the way, loneliness, helplessness and just
plain terror.

But on that sunny morning, the rest of my life seemed as
fresh and hopeful as when I was thirty, some forty years
ago. I have enough money for the time left and Grandmother helps me believe the future will be worth living.

She is my ex-mother-in-law, my forty-year-old son's
grandmother and one of my best friends. At ninety, she
makes me feel young. Looking into her contented, smiling
face with its snapping eyes, I forget my aches and pains, my
arthritis and inabilities, my dread of the future and my too-
frequent medical checkups in a search for what ails me and
know it is nothing, just normal development and ripening.

And I remember age is not only a frame of mind but a frame of reference as well. Grandmother is my reference point. I feel young and capable in her presence and can look forward to a future when I will spend my time savoring delicious memories.

On her flight North for her annual summer visit with friends and relatives, she had stopped off for a few days in Newberg, Ohio, arriving all dressed up and looking fresh as a daisy. We had had a nice family weekend and were both looking forward to our return to Michigan where Grandmother could "visit around" and I would begin serious retirement living. Grandmother likes to travel and we got off to a happy, bustling start on what was to prove an hilarious trip as she shared her memories of the past and her bright dreams of the future.

For a time we "spogged along" (her phrase) enjoying the scenery, the weather and even the trials of the turnpike, all the while keeping an eye out for likely places to stop for refreshment and to be refreshed, as she kept me entertained with her lively chatter and reminiscences.

Early in the trip she spied black smoke on the horizon and announced in gleeful excitement, "It must be a fire." (Grandmother always emphasizes the obvious and it does seem to add a certain zest to life.) At first we speeded up so she could see it burn, then slowed down so we would not miss it. She worried a bit, fearful it might go out before we could get there. But finally fortune smiled and we found it behind a restaurant oasis. When we stopped, she offered to buy ice-cream cones for us as a treat while we watched the fire.

Walking briskly to the "Ice-Cream Cones Only" section, she looked over the big cans of flavors in the glass-covered case and asked for "some of that caramel."

"That's fudge ripple," said the fellow ladling.

"Looks like caramel to me," said Grandmother correcting him.

"No, ripple," said the man.

"Well, all right, I'll take the ripple." She was still determined and added, "But it looks like caramel."

"Don't you think it looks like caramel?" she questioned the lady next in line.

"Yes," said the lady. "It sure does. I don't see much chocolate in it."

Gram seemed satisfied with this support, abandoned the argument and started digging in her purse for the forty-nine cents needed for a cone.

"I've just got to get rid of these nickels," she informed the man.

She dug busily away sorting out change. The man rested his elbow on the case and extended the cone which had begun to melt when Grandmother started digging. I offered to hold it so he could get on with his work but as I reached up, he jerked it back, looked at me threateningly and said menacingly, "It's hers." After some explanation, he relaxed his grip, gave me the cone, and Gram got to forty-nine cents.

"Well, dear, what are you going to have?" she sparkled, getting ready to dig again. I settled for chocolate. While I held the dripping ripple-caramel, Grandmother dug and counted, the man dipped and the next-in-line folks piled up.

Finally she finished, snapped her purse shut with its usual crash (it is a very good purse), retrieved her ripple and paid the man. I got my chocolate and we settled down beside the window to watch the fire which by now was only a few wisps of unspectacular smoke drifting up from an old strawstack.

Gram heaved a sigh, licked a bit and remarked, "My, wasn't that a lot to pay for a five-cent ice-cream cone?"

She was thinking of the past when cones were a nickel,

watching fires was exciting entertainment and people were fun. She looked at the smoldering straw and remarked, "I remember when Marvin Rapley burned Phil's strawstack. Just tossed a match in it and set it afire." She laughed.

"Yes," she went on, "Phil said he guessed he'd burn an old stack, so Marvin just tossed a match into it and set it afire."

Marvin was the family clown, a shirt-tail relative retired from railroading and a constant source of stories, unbelievable and joyous. Gram said he had his basement plumbed just like a steam locomotive hissing, spitting and dripping steam and water. He liked it that way and never fixed it as it reminded him of his days on the freights. He had a mule that wore a straw hat while pulling the garden cultivator and refused to move an inch if a fly got on his nose. Would just stop and turn around, look Marvin in the eye and wait for him to swat it off.

We sat and swapped yarns about Marvin and the family, licked our cones and enjoyed the fire which was again springing to life. Grandmother recalled the hunting story about Marvin and Phil. "You know," she went on, "Marvin said, 'Throw up your hat, Phil, and I'll shoot it.' Well, Phil pitched his hat in the air and Marvin shot it full of holes."

The yarns went on. We laughed together and ate down to the crisp cones by about the time she got to the story of how Marvin's wife moved out of their bedroom to one on another floor because of his trumpeting snore.

Deciding that people are not much fun anymore, we pushed on toward the next oasis for bathroom and snacks. It was quite a while before we stopped to phone ahead, report our progress and assure the Michigan relatives we were all right. Gram felt confident she "did not need to go" and offered to wait in the car while I went in. It was cool and quiet in the snack shop and business was slow. I approached the phone, certain a quick call would put us on our way.

Long distance calls from pay phones in various states all seem to be different so I got out my quarters, nickels and dimes, put on my glasses, scrooched down to eye level of the directions and carefully read:

"Put in 20¢—2 dimes or 1 dime and 2 nickels ..."

"Easy," I thought. "But a long distance call must surely be more complicated." I read on.

"For local calls, dial the number ..." That was not for me.

"For long distance calls in the area code, dial 1 and the number ..."

Not that either.

"For long distance calls outside the area, dial the area code + 0 + the number."

This was for me. But somewhere the "dial 1 + ..." had been left out.

As my telephoning experience began some sixty-five years ago when there was only one "crank" telephone in the neighborhood, which covered at least four square miles, and we had an understanding human "Central" to help us, I am not comfortable using automated, electronic instruments with complicated directions and tape-recorded messages which are only veiled threats as they correct my telephoning expertise.

I decided long distance must surely need a "1 + ..." so I deposited the necessary "20¢—2 dimes or 1 dime and 2 nickels ..." and dialed, "1 + 0 + ..." still feeling sure it must be correct. A metallic disembodied voice interrupted and chastised me severely: "We are unable to complete your call as dialed. Please hang up and dial again."

I dialed again "1 + 0 + ..." still feeling sure I was right.

Again, the strident message. The voice seemed abusive now and a bit petulant. I wondered if they built in the hurt tone. It made me feel I should apologize and assure someone I was not trying to damage the instrument.

By this time I had forgotten the number, as well as the instructions, but remembered my telephone credit card somewhere in the familiar jumble of my purse. I dug it out, readjusted my glasses and read the directions on the card. Not much help. It was for another state.

Getting a fresh start, I read all the directions again, put the " . . . 2 dimes or 1 dime and 2 nickels . . ." through the phone in another attempt to demonstrate my financial responsibility, tried leaving off the "1 + . . ." and experimented with "0 + the area code + the number . . ."

The voice said, "The number you have reached is not a listed number."

I knew this was not true. I was stuck. My resources in electronic communications were exhausted, I had lost all confidence in my ability to read and follow directions, had forgotten the number and needed to go to the bathroom, the doors to which stretched invitingly on my right (boy picture) and on my left (girl picture). Also, I had forgotten Grandmother still sitting in the hot car.

I tried again, rechecked the numbers and the instructions on the credit card, put in the " . . . 2 times—or 1 dime and 2 nickels . . ." dialed "0 plus the number . . ." and somehow got a person who took my credit card number, charged my call, returned my " . . . 2 dimes . . ." put me through to the anxious folks at home and seemed nice and friendly just like our "Central" person in the Old Days.

As I turned to go toward the girl door on the left to regain my composure, Gram entered at a brisk trot.

"My land, I've just got to go," she called as she dashed past me toward the boy door on the right.

"Left, left!" I screamed. Gram turned to better hear me, reversing right and left. I spun her around, shoved her left and dashed to the car to get the keys and lock it as we seemed to be in for a long spell what with bathrooms and lunch yet to go and probably more wondrous yarns.

Seating Gram in a cool booth, I began to eye the menu where it hung suspended high above the counter, decided against chicken salad and the hazard of botulism and thought she would probably like to have her old favorite, grilled cheese, which is easy to chew.

I approached the lunch counter person who seemed a combination of HRH Elizabeth Regina and a seven-foot Marine.

"I'd like a grilled cheese, please," I stammered knowing full well there was no grilled cheese posted.

"I'm sorry, Ma'am. We have not got any grilled cheese on the menu," she brusquely informed me.

I pointed a meaningful finger toward the "Grilled Cheese and Ham" thinking I had her cornered.

"No, Ma'am. No grilled cheese." She began to glare and waved her spatula ominously.

"OK. Just give me the Cheese and Ham and I'll take off the ham," I tried to coerce her into reason.

"We can't do that," she countered from behind the spatula. "I'm sorry, Ma'am."

She seemed truly contrite. Though I felt sure she was not only going to include the ham but make me eat it as well. Then she leaned across the counter, leered at me, and, as if she had me trapped, repeated, "Ma'am, we are not allowed to do that."

She knew she had me stopped as she quoted a higher authority. At least, it made me feel better to learn she had a higher authority to whom I might appeal. She turned her back and flipped two hamburgers. After finishing the hamburgers and delivering them to a customer, she continued to ignore me, doubtlessly feeling sure she had me adequately disposed of.

I stood my ground muttering, "A grilled cheese and two root beers," afraid she would forget and leave me stranded.

Finally, the counter person gave me a sneaky, sidelong glance from beneath her well-curled artificial eyelashes and sidled up to her next in command who was producing sandwiches. "She wants a grilled cheese," she confided to her companion *sotto voce*. The assistant turned to me questioningly, looking as if she had never heard of a grilled cheese.

"And two root beers," I warbled in my most pleasant tone. I was ready to swallow my pride, had lost my appetite and was worried about Gram.

Slowly, the next in command turned, plopped two slices of bread into a toaster, grabbed a piece of cheese, slammed it between the dry toast, quickly wrapped it and shoved it toward me without a word. I was not quite sure if she had put in the ham or not. I muttered again, "And two root beers, please," expecting the usual, "Small, medium or large?" inquisition. But, by now, I did not care.

I grasp my spoils and staggered toward Gram sitting unperturbed in the booth. She, at last, had her root beer and what could pass for a grilled cheese. I knew the rest of the trip home would be serene and interesting and no more vague directions and culinary ultimatums would harass me if I kept on driving and did not stop before we could unload her at her door.

I am grateful for her remembering and sharing her old family yarns, her inexhaustible sense of humor, her patience and understanding. But, most of all, I am grateful for every one of her ninety years she so graciously relives for us. And I look forward to more trips driving down the turnpikes in her beguiling company.

All my days cannot be as enchanting as the one with

Grandmother but they have meaning and are filled with experiencing and reminiscing in about equal portions. Retirement truly gives one time to savor the past, to laugh or cry about it as it may demand.

Since I left the school system, it has taken me several false starts and emotional detours to arrive at this comfortable apartment where I now find myself. The days drift by, each one lending its particular patina to a different way of life, now lived more or less only for me. Remaining family responsibilities and ties are loosed and self indulgence sets in. There is a sameness to all of my days, yet they go together to compile a pleasant, contemplative existence.

Each day's events remind me of times in the Old Days and, like the times now, they prove things do not change very much. If I should take those Old Days, just as they were, add some plumbing, electricity, paved roads, cars and traffic, toss in air pollution and world-wide electronic communication to help me keep my worries current, things are pretty much the same as they always were.

Getting old will take a lot of doing and getting used to. Somehow, I think it is going to be a lot of fun.

THE HAT

Monday, July 27.

This is a good time of year, when fall comes with lazy, quiet, rainy days sandwiched between the bright, busy ones. It arrives now, subtly and silently outside the windows and on the deck. I feel as though I could reach out and touch the softness of the day. Inviting and serene, it offers a balm to soothe the striving of summer.

The birds begin to flock. They no longer fly in pairs. Old mates and nests are forgotten and they all fly free with a new fall cry. It is a warning to prepare for the cold here or for the long trek South. The crows and the blue jays are the most raucous, defiant and jubilant. With no family cares, they fling themselves against the hazy sky and call out their freedom with nothing to do but eat, swoop, dip and swing in the endless air.

Everything is snuggling against the earth getting ready to sleep the long cold months away. The grass is brown. Some leaves fall in dry, yellow twirls. Weeds, in their endless and successful battle for survival, store the legacy of all their generations in the genes of every particle of their being: a bit of root, seeds to scatter, a leaf or piece of stem. They put to use whatever it takes to assure endless procreation as they travel in the digestions of unsuspecting animals, on the wind, in floods of rain and snow. They are forced to struggle—no one ever intentionally plants a weed.

And each spring they grow again, inviting shelter to wild things for nests and for food, for dried arrangements where they may at last be admired. Weeds are ingratiating as they bend down before hikers and hunters making a visible path to guide the way for a safe return. And when they spring up again, no one can tell where they bowed.

The days of each week blur. I do not remember what happened yesterday or the day before. Each morning stretches before me in an endless road, uninterrupted and empty, all the way to sunset and the evening news. I wonder how to fill it and hope someone will call. I procrastinate which can take a lot of time. I worry—very good for time consumption and very hard on the nerves. Anticipation? Very little of that in my days. Anticipation invites hopes and dreams. I try to think of some.

The trouble with hoping is that it demands a considerable expenditure of money. Hopes and dreams inevitably have to be nourished with a purchase. One cannot have hopes and save money too.

Still, they have always been a part of my life and brightened the long, dusty, hot, summer days on the Old Old Farm where we lived away out in the country before we moved to the Old Farm on the hill overlooking Hollandsville, the town in the valley where there were stores, a school and lots of people—most of them relatives. The arrival of Charley Burden's Grocery Wagon was one of our most exciting events and nourished about my oldest and fondest dream.

Charley's wagon was a beautiful little store on wheels, painted orange and trimmed with red. It had a curved roof and tiny curtained windows. The walls inside were lined with drawers and shelves that held everything a person would ever need to build a dream. Twice a week we heard him coming up our narrow country road, his wagon creaking and rattling and the horses' harness chank-chanking as he came carrying all the delights and necessities of life: groceries, hardware, shirts and shoes, pink wintergreen candies and hats—The Hat.

The Hat meant more to me than life itself and every time Charley came by I rushed out to the road, stretched my six-year-old legs to climb the back steps of his wagon and squeezed down the narrow aisle between the shelves and drawers to make sure The Hat had not been bought and carried away by somebody who had money.

It was straw, a beautiful bright yellow straw with a wide brim and right smack-dab in the middle was a bunch of shiny red cherries with green leaves held by a bit of purple ribbon. Often, I completely ignored Charley's pink wintergreen candies to stand staring at The Hat while I fed my soul and forgot my stomach. I was sure that with The Hat on my head, life truly would be beautiful. I could imagine walking along wearing it, swaying a little to make the cherries rattle and enjoying the jealous, longing looks of the town cousins who bought things at the stores on Main Street and would never know the joys of a grocery wagon like Charley's

I never thought of asking for The Hat. Mother and Grandmother were always busy buying needles and buttons, underwear and shirts, flour and sugar—strictly necessities. There never was money for dreams, only necessities. Then, as now, dreams meant dollars.

All summer long The Hat beckoned me every time Charley stopped by our house. No one ever seemed to notice when I blocked the aisle and stood looking at its glory until the very last minute. Only when he climbed up on the seat that stretched across the front of his wagon, released the brake, slapped the reins, clucked to the horses and shouted, "Giddy yap," did I rush to the back and jump down the steps. Then I stood in the middle of the road and watched him disappear over the hill carrying all my hopes for achieving a life of glamour and meaning.

So far as I know, no one ever bought The Hat. Perhaps no one else ever imagined its possibilities. I was glad and relieved. Even then, I suspicioned it was better to dream about the enhancement of The Hat than to wear it and find it did not make the town cousins jealous and who probably would only have laughed at me anyway. I could almost hear them sniggering as they poked each other in the ribs and mocked, "There goes Henny in her mother's hat."

But The Hat has never been forgotten. It was always a dream and, like all really good, worthwhile dreams and hopes, it has stayed that way. I came to realize that, if I was to keep the dream, I could never wear The Hat.

GOING "OUT"

Monday, August 3.

Vicious summer is back. I tire of it, urge the season on its way and dream of cold weather. Winters on both of the Old Farms were a time of great apprehension but they still had a certain *joie de vivre* as we worked to combat all the weather threw at us with every expediency we could contrive.

Before indoor plumbing, "going out" during wind and rain, snow and ice, hot sun and blizzards demanded our most cunning innovation. Father, proud and more concerned with modesty than with convenience, hid the privy as far away from the house as possible, making it necessary for everyone to anticipate physical needs far in advance in order to "get out" in time.

On the Old Old Farm, it stood within easy access to the back door. Grandmother Dorset had had it placed there many years back and Father never did dare change it. But, by the time we moved to the Old Farm on the hill overlooking town where the relatives lived with their indoor toilets, we became more sedate and did not wish anyone to know we lacked such a convenience. So Father put it at the end of a long journey past the wood pile, along the side of the chicken coop, around the corner of the coop, and there, out of sight, he hid the "outhouse." It was a three-holer and a great socializer. Especially at night, for nobody wanted to take the lantern and face the long, velvet-black trip alone.

In order to manage the traffic to and fro, one usually announced before departing, "I'm going out," or sometimes, to a person of the same sex, "Do you want to go out with me?"

Being the only girl in the family, I usually went out by myself unless I was lucky enough to have a guest. At night, it was a long, dark, lonely trip with the lantern casting its feeble, flickering, yellow glow in a circle around my feet. As I walked past the side of the chicken coop, it threw my shadow up against the wall twenty feet high with my legs waving underneath like branches in the wind. I could get marvelously weird results by swinging the lantern violently back and forth. The activity took my mind off the ominous night and gave me courage so that I almost forgot to be afraid. I wondered if swinging it in an arc overhead would turn the whole shadowy world upside down. But such experimentation was for my brave brothers, not for me. I knew I could get spattered with kerosene, put out the lantern, and be left alone in the dark.

We never seemed to think much about the dark. It was part of our lives like wind and rain and green apples, Grandmother's lemon pie and trees to climb. Just another of the adventures of farm life, some times enjoyed, sometimes dreaded. So, at the end of the trip by lantern light, accompanied by my thoughts, lots of bugs in summer and bright snowy shadows in winter, I arrived at the outhouse.

There is a technique to going out in order to obtain the greatest comfort and least inconvenience. In summer, leave the lantern outside if you do not want to sit amid a million light-loving insects. In winter, sit down, set the lantern on the floor between your feet, lean forward and hunch your coat up over your shoulders to make a nice warm tent. Then, if you do not prove to be too combustible and immolate yourself, you can relax and feel snug and secure.

After the long trip and all the preparation, excretion, although it brought relief, was sort of an anticlimax and was always accompanied by thoughts of doing a good job, for it was unpleasant contemplating another trip through the night and the weather. That was the exhortation when you were small—some adult crouching down beside you pleading, almost demanding, "Now do a good job. I'm not going to bring you out here again tonight." Mind set and human physiology being what they are, such a threat usually resulted in the smallest, least significant job possible, which meant you would have to request another escort or use the pot.

The Pot. It was sort of a regal title—never just pot but The Pot. Grandmother was more refined. She called it "The Slop Jar." Every night it stood in the cold upstairs hall within easy access of all who were in need, or who were too young to go downstairs, feel their way along in the dark to the cold kitchen, find a match and light the lantern, bundle up and take the long journey past the woodpile, along the side of the chicken coop and around the corner to the outhouse. Some of Father's pride and modesty must surely have rubbed off on us for no one ever gave up and said, "What's the use? It isn't worth it," and used the back yard, chicken yard or barn yard.

The Pot was empty, shining clean, white and inviting as it stood there in the hall at bedtime. It even smelled good for

Grandmother was scrupulous about putting a little soap-suds in its bottom to disinfect it. But, with five kids and three adults, it was full and foul by morning. The wise ones got to it early before it started to fill. Using it later required some prudence: look at its level, judge your own capacity before squatting on its cold, hard, narrow rim, then be careful not to sit so your bottom stuck too far down into its depths. It was always quite possible to fill it so far you ended up squatting in cold pee.

If you were lucky, it was only pee. Filling The Pot with anything else was frowned upon. There was not any hate like that held for someone who grunted in The Pot in order to avoid the long trip "out." Grunting was for day—night was only for peeing.

However, with dexterity and sound judgment as to how full The Pot was, and how much fuller it would be when you finished, you could be quite comfortable, relax, finish up, scrub your nightgown around a little to wipe off the excess, scoot back to bed and sleep soundly, when, if you were fortunate, you would not need to "go out" until morning.

It is surely a credit to our judgment and consideration for each other that The Pot never did run over, nor did anybody ever stumble in the dark and spill it there in the cold upstairs hall. So far as I know, my brothers always managed to "hit the pot." Though there in the pitch black night it does appear to have required considerable skill and some planning.

It was years before we had recovered enough from the Depression to acquire inside plumbing. All that time The Pot served our needs with efficiency and some degree of grandeur and luxury. Anything that saved us the long, though fascinating journey necessary to "go out" was truly a luxury. For luxury is not what a thing may be, but how much better it is than the alternative.

NO SLACKS IN CHURCH

Monday, August 17.   The month

goes racing along toward September, fall and the cold winter. Today it seems to have made it—only forty-seven degrees last night. Clear and cool this morning. There were stars visible bright above the parking lot floodlights. Andromeda moves up over the apartment building across the street. I got up early to look out the back bedroom window at the sky. It was lovely. The Pleiades wink their way into my peripheral vision. The moon phases along with the passing days. They are old friends and keep me company during my old-lady wakeful times.

Yesterday was a good day, cool and cloudy. Put on my new blue suit and my old pink blouse and went to church in Negamo, the neighboring village where I lived for years. With so many of us vacationing, we meet with the Presbyterians this summer in order to have a respectable congregation. Church breaks up a lonely day and makes me feel I can chuck my responsibilities on the Lord, breathe a sigh of relief and get off to a new start by making some good, solid, utilitarian resolutions. It is good practice for trying out clothes and generally getting life in order. Discovered today that I can squeeze my flattened out summer feet into heels and walk without falling down.

Old age might easily become deadly dull with no contacts, no one to talk with, no reason for dressing up, no place to go for any purpose. Days go by. I talk to shop people and myself and wish there was someone around who could lift one end of a conversation or just be here to slam doors and litter. Wonder if that is the reality of old age: becoming more and more isolated until one is completely alone and everything ends. Maybe one just gets so tired it is good to go.

Saw Lara Widmore at church. She is a local monument. Recovered from whatever disabled her last year and looks only about fifty of her eighty years. Lara belongs to one of the old local families who settled Negamo and she still owns a lot of it. She owns a lot of the church too. Her gifts are magnificent but never mentioned. She just keeps on giving as a way of continuing the family effort. As the area has been pretty well pioneered, peopled, built up and subdivided, there is not much left of real pioneering to do, so she expands the church. It is nice.

Originally, much like that long-ago town sitting in the valley below our Old Farm, Negamo existed for generations to serve only the needs of its people and the country around. But, like so many pleasant and inviting communities, it has grown too fast and matured too soon. For a century or more it sat on the edge of the city, quiet and content, a lot of farms and a few stores at the four corners to serve all our needs. People walked across the fields, fished from the riverbanks and talked to each other.

Then subdivision struck and we were a town no more. Developers bought the land we so eagerly sold to them, covered it with ranch-type houses and apartments, threw in some low-cost housing to satisfy societal and financing requirements, and started computing depreciation and tax write-offs.

All the people who wanted country living moved into the ranch-type houses, the apartments and the low-cost housing and began to consume the buildings, the land and the social life of the community. No one knew anyone any more. We quit talking and walking—too much traffic moving too fast for walking and talking. Most who still walked on our once quiet country roads were run off. A few were hit, some were killed. Everything was being used up with nothing put back to nourish the community and a way of life.

Nowhere was it more evident than in our church. The back door became the front door. No room to park in the front anymore. The road had to be widened to accommodate the Sunday shoppers hurrying to the Mall that had been thrown up to "supply the needs of the area." There is something about going to church that postulates an Entrance, a place to enter a house of worship. Now we sneaked and streaked around in back to crowd into an inadequate parking lot sandwiched between the back of the church and the front of the Mall.

The people changed. They deteriorated like the building. No one dressed up for church. They came in slacks and wore no hats. Hats at church were once a joy. One could sit high in the balcony close to Heaven and gaze over a magnificent display of vanity and pride. Now, when the service dragged, there was nothing to look at but a lot of hair.

And hair is hair. All pretty much the same except for length and shade—or lack of. All the ribbons and simulated flowers and birds were gone. Just a sea of heads was left, all pretty dull. Who can ponder on the magnificence of Heaven while observing a sea of hair?

Now the town is being eaten up. "Urban decay" they call it. It is not decay, it is consumption. The community is being ingested by economic and social appetites leaving behind only the excrement of their voraciousness. But there is hope. The new people will move on when they have exhausted everything. A few folks will be left and become new pioneers to build again. And then, some other appetite will come one day, move in, enjoy the pleasant living and open space and consume again.

So Lara, and all like her, are saving some of our past and building a new future. Through her love and her gifts, the back of the church is being turned into an Entrance. Its inside is becoming gracious and beautiful. People begin to talk though there is not much of any place to walk yet. Lara will probably make one somewhere in a lovely spot.

In the meantime, she drives all of her magnificent years to church in her well-preserved old Chrysler and appears each Sunday, always a gentle and firm reminder of how things should be. She is our monument. She will preserve us.

And she does not wear slacks to church.

NIGHT WORK

Monday, August 24. Summer,

hot, muggy summer is back. I dream of fall. It seems impossible, but sometimes I look forward to cold air to breathe, snow to crunch under foot and spring to hope for. Four big crows flew past the deck this morning in the hot dusty air. Low to the ground, they flapped between the buildings cawing in conversation as they looked over possibilities for winter foraging from the barbecue remains left on lawns and decks. Crows are wise. They plan.

There is a special smell to each season: new-turned earth in the spring, cold, nose-puckering winter, green growing things in summer. Fall smells like everything that has accumulated all summer long: dry grass, the special, specific smells forced out of buildings and fields by hot sun and dust, rotting fruit and vegetables lying about forgotten in a time of plenty, weeds with their insistent, penetrating odor to punctuate your olfactory and water your eyes and the satisfying smell of fallen leaves that crunch and rattle underfoot, then get soggy when it rains, sending up a message of the coming cold and a promise of spring. Dead leaves smell like hope.

I remember fall on the farm, the Old Farm, the one we moved to after we had all been born and had grown enough to begin helping with the work. It was a glorious hurrying time—hurrying to get ready for the start of school and to get the garden vegetables stored away. "Getting the garden in" was a celebration of plenty, not a chore. Everything had its special time for gathering and its special place for storing. We did it with exuberance because it was exciting. Mother made it exciting with intent. She would have made a great general.

Mother watched for the first frost in order to let things grow as long as possible, but still grab them in before they froze, which usually meant night work. As the days cooled and shortened, she cast her practiced eye at the late afternoon sky and announced, "We better get the potatoes and cabbages in tonight, it's going to freeze." This required the use of the Old Ford. There was no other kind in those Depression days. No one we knew ever had a new one.

Mother commenced her round-up of all the available labor force by doing a lot of calling and walking. She liked best to start walking and calling on the theory that she could call ahead, be heard and heeded, thus saving the remainder of her walk. Not, "Albert, Hubert, David and Daniel," the twins. And the most ridiculous of all, "Henrietta." None of us had a name with long vowels that carried well so she put an "ie" on the end of each one: "Bertie, Pewee," for Hubert as he was the tallest kid of us all, "Davy, Danny and Henny." Very often Henrietta became, "Henry" and I was to wear that masculine name all my life.

On a smelly, hazy, fall afternoon, her call, which she had developed into a sort of yodel to make it carry farther, reached us where we were sitting on the wild grape-covered rock pile at the end of the lane smoking grapevine cigarettes, in the woods exploring, in the swamp climbing up to look in the heron's nest or chasing the chicken-robbing skunk that lived in the pasture under a big rock.

I never remember answering her, but I surely remember the carrying call. It floated above the shimmering summer heat and seemed to be transported on the fall smells. She was intensely serious about being able to call so it would carry a long way and delighted in having me practice "Yoo Hoo!" She emphasized that I should sing out the "ooo" part in order to get the greatest distance.

I often stood in front of the woodshed trying out my adolescent voice over the back yard and dwelling on the vowels, not letting the consonants choke me as I hollered through the top of my head. It made me a little dizzy but taught me something about vowels, consonants and resonance. I became quite expert and looked about for someone to summon.

Once, emerging from the kitchen door to round up my brothers, I let out a near perfect "Yoo Hooo!" that could have been heard at least a mile. Instead, it landed smack on the ears of a charming somewhat "older kid" who had come to visit. He looked astonished, turned and walked straight back down the driveway to the road. I was not sure if he had come to see me and often wondered. And my "Yoo-Hoooing!" days came to a sudden, mute halt. Stopped cold by social awareness.

As soon as Mother got us all together, we began getting the Old Ford ready for hauling vegetables. Bertie, already growing into the engineer he eventually became, got the trailer ready. Where the trailer had come from no one knew. It was part of our culture, inherited along with old family portraits, snapshots, beautiful linens and cold remedies. It must have been contrived by some thoughtful progenitor and preserved by Mother and Father as being necessary for our subsistence. Bertie toggled it up—it always needed fixing—hitched it behind the Old Ford and we were ready to "go to the garden."

But first, the late afternoon chores had to be done. A thousand chickens fed and their eggs gathered, the pigs "slopped," and cows "got up" and all the farm readied for the night.

We started with the chickens as they went to bed very early. "Chook, chook, chook," we called while we scattered grain. Why the "Chook, chook, chook," no one knew, except Mother called "Chook, chook, chook," and Grandmother called "Chook, chook, chook." And like the vowels in our names, it carried better than "Chicken, chicken, chicken," which sounds pretty silly anyway, besides not carrying. That was the way with our speech, our manners and mode of life. Everything had a purpose and the purpose contributed to our survival.

Emerging from the acrid smell of the chicken yard, my next chore was slopping the pigs. I enjoyed feeding the pigs. They are such enthusiastic eaters. The mixture of garbage and middlings smelled appetizing and good. The slops started with our all-purpose ten-quart pail full of peelings from the day's potato paring, vegetable and fruit canning, leftover meals and some skim milk from the cream separator. Then I added a few handfuls of middlings, a mixture of finely ground grains, soft and cool to the touch and smelling, along with the garbage, like some delicious kind of muffin. Mixing it up with a piece of an old, narrow board released all the accumulated, nose-tantalizing smells of the day and made me realize why the pigs seemed to enjoy their food so much.

By the age of ten or so, I could carry two pails full of

slops out to the pigs in the old shed, climb into the pen and dump the stuff into the trough while standing on one foot and kicking away the hungry, eager pigs with the other. "Slurrpchompt, slurp, chompt, chompt," the pigs started gulping almost before the food hit the trough, forcing me to dump a lot on their ears and snouts.

It was a good sound and smell there in the pigpen in the cool shed. Pigs do not sweat and are really not dirty, just vicious. Past experiences had taught me that their bites were painful and, from Mother's recounting of poor Uncle Tom in Mrs. Stowe's now put-aside novel, pigs would eat anything including me.

Somehow, it never bothered me about poor Uncle Tom. The story was vaguely exciting and scary, but unreal. I had had it drummed into me that I was never to fall down in the pigpen because, like Uncle Tom, I would be eaten. I was not frightened, but kept on my guard and knew that as long as the pigs had slops, they would not want me. Nevertheless, I was careful not to fall while landing effective kicks on their fat sides. The technique of balancing and kicking while pouring and whacking the last of the peelings out of the pail was more interesting than matters of life and death as I enjoyed the sounds and smells of slopping the pigs.

Bert and Pewee readied the cows for milking. It was a leisurely chore, making a trip to the end of the lane where the cows pastured in the back field. First, they whistled up Gussie who had grown up with us and knew more about going to get the cows than we did, took their "bull-whacker" down from where it hung handy in the cowbarn on the wall behind the stalls and started down the lane. The bull-whacker, like the trailer, had its origin in our immediate needs and was used to separate Watsinger's bull from our herd of cows.

Somewhere deep in the woods on the line between our

land and Watsinger's, there was a hole in the boundary fence, the location of which only the bull knew and no one else ever bothered about. As he came and went, our cows frequently birthed calves resembling Watsinger's herd a lot more than our own and they often made pointed remarks about "free use of our bull." No one ever took time to fix the fence. The boys just carried their bull-whacker for protection and farm life went on in its nonchalant, dangerous way.

"Don't run the cows," Mother called after their retreating figures. She might have added, "Don't ride them." But what she did not know was always to our advantage. We were not deceitful, just prudent.

Riding a cow is quite a challenge. There is nothing to hang onto as with a horse that has a nice, handy, long-haired mane to grip and expects to be ridden anyway. Staying on a cow required a lot of dexterity, determination and the ability to fall off without landing on the stones that lined the lane. I tried a few times but was always better at falling off than staying on. Bertie had it all figured out. He got off before coming in sight of the house.

After bringing up the cows and sending them at a gallop with full bags swinging and squirts of milk flying from bulging teats as they trotted eagerly but silently over the barn door sill and into their respective stalls, the next chore was feeding them hay and ground grain.

When the hay had been stuffed down from the haymow overhead and the grain put in the feed boxes of the stalls, we left them to eat while waiting for Father to end his day of working in the fields and come up to do the milking. Supper finished, we all piled into the Old Ford and started for the garden three fields back the lane where an especially fertile acre or so had been plowed near a little dew-pond to furnish us water in times of drought.

On the trip down the lane, the empty trailer bounding and banging behind us, Mother firmly grasped the Old Ford's steering wheel and eased us over the stones and ruts and across the field to the garden where we arrived about dark. She parked so the car lights shone down the vegetable rows and Us Kids began to dig potatoes and gather cabbages. In our cheery patch of light, we danced about flipping potatoes out of the sandy soil with expert twists of the manure fork and chopping off cabbage heads. We had no thought of the big darkness around us or that we were working at night.

Work went quickly for we were highly motivated. The farther we got down the rows from the headlights of the Old Ford, the farther we could throw the cabbages to get them into the trailer. There was a lot of competition between us and with ourselves. It was a matter of pride to excel our own best past effort in everything we did. We continually tried to improve; throwing cabbages, riding cows, kicking hogs, making grapevine cigarettes which would really smoke and skating on thin ice without falling through. There was subtle, fun-loving trickery involved too, as we hurried to get a long way down the rows in order to improve our throwing skills before Mother noticed us and moved the car.

She walked along beside us while we dug and cut and threw, picking up potatoes and putting them in gunnysacks, filling them only full enough for us to lift while she watched the inventive skill of her children with quiet pride. Mother was not a dexterous worker, but she truly admired the ability in others. She thought in terms of the arts and literature for which she had been schooled long before farm work and children claimed all her time and energy.

She noticed my efficient potato digging and flipping and remarked, "It's like music to see how you do that with such a rhythm." I had done it intentionally and was proud of my skill. But my greater concern was to have Mother recognize it and for her to tell me so.

Late in the evening when we had finished, we all piled into the Old Ford and Mother managed to coax it to pull the loaded trailer out of the soft garden soil, across the field and back down the lane to the house. Everything had to be put away. The potatoes could wait through the dark night until morning but would have to go into the cellar quickly before the light turned them green. We knew from an early age that a green potato quickly rots. And there is nothing worse than the way a rotten, green potato feels and smells when you grab into it while hunting around in the dark cellar bin getting some up for supper.

The resting place for cabbages was a deep hole beneath the North Porch reached through an enormous trap door. Every head had to be wrapped in newspaper. Newspapers were useful in those days, the ink did not come off on anything: cabbages, wet clothes, fresh baked cookies and meat. Then more throwing and pitching to develop muscles and dexterity and the cabbages were moved quickly into the cool, earthen root cellar beneath the porch floor.

Our only light was an oil lamp set on a table far from the operation. We all knew what would happen if we knocked over a lamp. Even if it did not explode, it would start a fire and burn the house down anyway. So our throwing skills became expert as we avoided the lamp and sent the cabbages flying into the winter's food storage.

At last they would be put away and the Old Ford left with its trailerload of potatoes to wait for another day. Then we all trudged out in the darkness to the well, pumped water over our dirty feet, got a long, cool drink and turned toward bed. Another of our days would have come to its late-evening end. Outside of running the cows to watch the milk fly and riding them, a few smokes of wild grapevine on the cool, shady stonepile at the end of the lane, the joy of running, pitching, competing and trying to improve, the day, as all others, was pretty much work.

We had fun.

A FINAL GOOD-BYE

Monday, August 27.   I must be

settling into retirement. I like staying home to fuss around at unimportant tasks, sorting, rearranging and experimenting, to dig out old closets and cupboards and find things so long forgotten they seem new. It is like Christmas or an extra birthday.

It would be nice to be an old woman hermit and sit quietly here at home to create and do little else but listen to the weather; the way the wind sounds blowing the chimes on the deck, whistling around the windows, soughing in the pines outside the back bedroom and sometimes, rain spanking down. Even sleet is nice for listening.

It is a joy to get up in the morning and sit to watch God make the day—particularly nice now. He does not start so early. I can stagger out to the kitchen for an early cup of coffee, curl up in the big, soft chair, sit sipping and watch the day come. I marvel that He can find such a variety of beginnings for days: new sky colors and cloud shapes, changing temperatures, barometric pressures and winds, changing light and humidity. Then He throws a bunch of birds up against the sky and adds a late rabbit hurrying across the lawn after a night's frisking. Alice's rabbit must have been for real. He hurried too. Rabbits always run as if they were late but were not sure for what or to where.

This has been a good week for social endeavor, meeting family obligations and do-gooding. Monday was to have been go-to-Detroit day with Adah to see her daughter-in-law, Laurane, and the kids. Laurane was too tired for company so Adah switched projects, called to inform me and asked, "Don't you want some of this corn I picked to take to Detroit?"

Corn for the coming cold winter seemed good so I said, "I'll be out in about forty-five minutes," and hurried out to Adah's spacious country place. She had not only picked the corn but husked it as well and packed it in a steamer all ready to "do up." All in forty-five minutes! It bothered me, somehow, to see she had picked exactly enough to fill the steamer, with all the ears packed neatly on end as though they were absolutely eager to shed their kernels and hop into the freezer.

Before I came home, we took a trip to the grocery store, had a cup of coffee, exchanged a few conjectures on the state of the family and international politics (Adah is a deep thinker) and I got started for home loaded with her generous gift.

Evening came moseying along and just as I had finished steaming corn, cutting it off cobs, packing, putting to freeze and had laid my exhausted self down to enjoy a few minutes' respite with Tuchman's *A Distant Mirror*, the phone jingled.

"Laurane called and said we could come tomorrow," Adah informed me. I had rather expected it and was ready.

"I'm going out and pick again." she went on. "I don't suppose there's much left and it's probably too big."

Guilt gripped me at having taken the Detroit-bound corn. But I felt sure she would prowl up and down the rows of her glorious garden and come up with four dozen great ears.

On Friday, we went to Detroit to see Laurane who is dying of lung cancer. It is remarkable how the family accepts impending death. It is as though the first awareness tears a great bleeding gash in us as we begin to suffer. Then after a while, we close ranks over the wounds of shock and grief, take comfort in each other, accept what is to be and go on doing the best we can at whatever has to be done. The routine of living takes over and pushes aside the hurt. Corn gets picked and canned, cooking and cleaning and even fun detract us from sadness. It is a kind of selfishness that heals our wounds and lifts us up.

Laurane accepts the ending of her life, knowing other lives will go on for her husband and their five children and for our family. She is a realist and it gives her strength.

She is trying to get everything in order while there is time. The little kids into school, one blind and beautiful daughter enrolled in college, the oldest girl's wedding planned, her youngest son's incipient bone cancer operated on and the minutiae of her own life ordered. She spends quiet times with her husband. They make ultimate plans and enjoy doing things that would otherwise have been for a later time. The things they had planned to do sometime, they do now.

We three go to lunch, Adah, Laurane and I. As we settle down in a booth, Laurane says, "Thanks for helping me to get away from the kids for a while." It is difficult for her, these last good-byes. She needs some adult conversation. Food is her panacea and she orders a big strawberry shortcake.

"I want the last rites," she offers with no apropos. "Haven't been to church for twelve years, but the social worker is trying to find me a priest who will give them to me."

Adah raises her head and stops in mid-bite to remind her, "I thought you were excommunicated when you had the birth control operation." Adah is a realist, too, and knows we have to face facts.

We finished lunch in a desultory fashion and return to the house and the kids. As Adah and I start for home, there is nothing to say but, "Good-bye." Somehow it carries a special and final meaning.

September

FUN ON THE RIVER

Wednesday, September 2.

Finally, we have rain. It has come down steadily all through the past week. We needed it to make the season seem right.

Went out with Bert and Adah for supper last night. In a futile attempt at reducing, I asked for Weight Watchers toast and cottage cheese. After serving us, the waiter person looked at me and announced, "No cottage cheese."

"What do you suggest?" I asked hopefully.

He looked blank and seemed to have become mute.

"Applesauce," called the Assistant Manager, who was clearing the table in the next booth.

"OK, applesauce," I agreed.

The waiter did not respond. I watched for a time while he hunted here and there and finally fumbled over to the salad bar where he found the applesauce and brought it to me quite triumphantly with no spoon. As I had been supplied with a knife and fork, the fellow seemed to feel that was enough. But he stood by the table solicitously while I stared at the applesauce and finally asked, "Would you like a spoon?" as if he was truly concerned.

"Yes. That would be nice. I surely would like a spoon," I replied, entertaining visions of eating the sauce with a fork.

The spoon came. The toast came. I tried to eat slowly to convince myself it would serve as dinner. It didn't. And as I nibbled, I thought about how strange it is that I seem to have so many problems in restaurants.

We three chatted contentedly about the world in general, decolleté necklines, the starting of school and our children. Along about dusk, Bert and Adah dropped me off at home in a gathering evening thunderstorm.

Yesterday afternoon was a relaxed and happy time at brother Dave's. I drank tea, refused a bacon and tomato sandwich and came home laden with garden "sass" as Uncle Charley called it.

He was one of the great eaters of the family. Alone most of his adult life, he filled his days with gardening, cooking and eating. And he never gained an ounce. His wife, Aunt Lorinda, died of cancer after only a few years of their marriage and Charley lived from then on with her sister, beautiful Aunt Deborah.

Mother repeatedly explained to me, "Aunt Deb is Uncle Charley's housekeeper," lest I become too inquisitive as to why they were not married. Adults too often explain things ahead of time in an effort to ward off a difficult kid question. It had never occurred to me to ask about it. They were Aunt Deb and Uncle Charley and went together as naturally as apple pie and cheese, a combination to make us all feel comfortable and cared for. Now, I wonder. The generations do not change so much. The arrangements and relationships of today seem mirrored in the past.

After Aunt Deb died, Uncle Charley stayed alone in the big house in Hollandsville until the folks decided, "Charley can't stay alone winters anymore." So it was arranged that we should leave the farm during winter and move into town to keep him company in the warm house next to the school. Each fall and spring for years, Willie Diplown and his helpers picked up all our belongings and moved us. We moved so often we became as mobile as a circus and had as much fun as if we were one.

The move into town each fall gave us a brief release from the cold farmhouse on the hill and a lift up the social ladder. We felt that we, at last, were on an equal footing with the relatives who lived in town and not just country cousins anymore. We became the only family around to have both a summer and a winter home.

Uncle Charley's house was a mammoth place: a front parlor, living room, dining room, kitchen, back kitchen (pump room) and lots of porches. It had three bedrooms and only one closet. There was an indoor toilet tucked into a nook at the head of the cellar stairs. Just a stool, no lavatory, no tub and no locking door.

The door must have been retrieved from some ancient parlor to be put to a more practical use. It had fancy quilted glass forming the top half of its surface and swung both ways. You could go in or out without unlatching it as it had no knob. But the "convenience" was comfortable and cozy and certainly better than our far away "double-u-see" which father's sense of modesty had made him place so far out behind the chicken coop. In spite of its lack of privacy, the arrangement gave us a great sense of security and elegance to know we did not have to wade through snowbanks and battle blizzards just to "go out." For years, it served the eight of us with grace and comfort. Like the rest of the house, it was warm and inviting.

We all especially delighted in the continuous welcome heat that came from the big furnace in the cellar which was fueled with wood chunks gathered from the farm. They were about eighteen-inch long slices of tree trunks each weighing around twenty pounds when green, fifteen or so dry, and had to be split in order to give off good heat. I learned to do it almost before I was twelve, probably because I was always cold. No one ever taught me. I just found out by watching Father or my brothers. That was the way we learned on the farm: watching someone or experimenting because we were cold or tired or hungry. It made us eager learners and effective innovators.

Wood-chunk-splitting was pretty simple once you found out that the chunks would split better from one end than they would if chopped from the other. You just stood them on end on the cellar floor, grabbed the axe, put it behind you in order to get a good, full swing, swung it around up over your head and whacked down putting all your weight behind it. Giving the axe a slight twist just as it hit would usually result in the satisfying crack of two pieces coming apart and flying away across the floor. If it didn't, you turned the chunk end for end and tried again.

I did not have much weight but had developed a good full swing and it was a particular joy for me to split furnace chunks. As usual, I never felt it was work, only a good way to improve my technique. It was a game like the golf and tennis we had heard about that needed a good full swing and follow through. Somehow, the axe seemed better and more fun. Perhaps because it was patently more dangerous. It made us feel superior.

The only sports in town were football and baseball played down on the River Flats behind the Post Office. Often flooded and wet, they were only for those few lusty, gifted athletes from the farms around who were on The Team. So we took refuge in the sour grapes of wood-splitting. Maybe that is why the house was always so comfortable—we all liked to split wood and boast about how good we were at it.

After we moved in to keep Uncle Charley company, he fixed himself an apartment out of a few extra rooms which had been roosting on one side of the living room. In them he put all the relics of his life: his violin, his collection of seashells and dried sponges from a 1920 automobile trip to Florida, his books and writing materials, wood-working tools, garden seeds and his onions. Winters he fiddled, cooked and ate his onions, wrote his poems and fixed things with his tools. Summers he raised vegetables to keep us well fed through the long, hungry winters. He did not take time to read his books—just kept them; for a book is a treasure never to be thrown away.

He never neglected his poems. An occasional printing in the *Hollandsville News* or the inclusion of one in a family funeral oration kept him inspired. They were like his conversation, gently reproving and critical of new gadgets and the changing social order.

He wrote about the passing of The Good Old Days, the Russo-Japanese War, the lovely ladies he had known, the fun of hog butchering on the farm and the dangers of too much dependence on gasoline. As early as 1920, he wrote:

MY LADY GASOLINE

> *There's a despot rules o'er all this land*
> *O'er all this land today*
> *No tyrant grim of olden time*
> *Held more despotic sway*
> *All up this land and down this land*
> *There rules this erstwhile queen*
> *All bow the kings and homage pay*
> *To my lady gasoline.*

There's trouble enough comes to us all
As we tramp this vale of tears
Don't seek to any burdens add
To your declining years
And, if in quiet you should wish
To pass life's closing scene
Don't listen to the siren call I pray
Of any gas machine.

Charley often gave the impression that he was writing about "other folks." But he was not a dispassionate man. He led a vigorous life, deeply concerned with the world and everything in it: lost loves and wars and just plain deviltry.

He carefully printed each poem in a sturdy, hardcover notebook that has endured to remind us of his dreams and concerns in that long-ago time. In his writing he preserved the past and gave us a gift that cautions, "Don't forget." Gone from us for a long time now, he is yet with us in his poems.

His fiddle was very special. He had salvaged it from some family attic and remodeled it to accommodate his broad fingertips years of woodworking in Dawn's furniture factory had damaged until they were too blunt to fit the strings. He spent a lot of time redesigning its neck, restringing it and anxiously trying it out. Then he would redo it and try again with such scraping and squawking the tunes were lost and only the rhythm remained. He spent more time perfecting his design than he did producing music, which he never seemed to care too much about, for he was quite deaf and viewed the world with a certain detachment, only admitting the things he wished to hear. He was happy with the rhythm and the words he mumbled in a monotone as he sawed away while he ignored the melodies.

It was always the same old songs: "I Danced With The Girl With A Hole In Her Stocking" and "Buffalo Gals, Ain't You Comin' Out Tonight?" No matter what the words, the tunes all sounded alike.

Charley drove Mother crazy. In the evenings when he was full of boiled onions and contentment, he got out his fiddle and filled the whole big house with his foot-stomping old songs and rhythms.

"Charley is fiddling again," Mother would announce. I wonder that she noticed him above the din of five children and all their friends gathered for an evening of family fun.

Or, she would sniff and say, "Charley is boiling onions again." Charley always seemed to be doing things "again." Never, to my knowledge, did he ever to anything for the first time. He just went on and on fiddling and cooking and eating and writing, raising flowers and vegetables and doing everything he could to keep us healthy and happy.

Charley never appeared to get older, a gentle soft-spoken, slightly fumbling man in old black clothes and very determined ways. He had white hair and a white mustache. His face was not impressive. It held a quiet dignity that had nothing to do with the shape of his features. You felt his warm personality and enjoyed his kindness without thinking about how he looked. I mostly remember him for what he did, not for his mien. He was a presence in our lives. Without him, we would have been incomplete.

He always looked the same except when he got dressed up for Lodge in his Odd Fellows uniform with his sword and his hat with the beautiful white ostrich feather plumes. As he went off, sober and dignified and quite gallant, he was not the Uncle Charley we knew at all but a man with all the attributes of maleness.

Once a week he was quite sexy when he left the house in all his splendor. We felt we were losing him. Lodge was the only part of his life he did not share with us and we were forever afraid he might not come back.

But in the morning, we would hear him busy in his apartment fixing things and cooking. As the fumes of his boiled onions penetrated the house and all the yard around, we sighed in contented security knowing he was all ours for another week. Someone would exclaim, "Uncle Charley is back," and the delightful, dependable sameness of our lives would go on.

The only thing that ruffled Charley was some of Us Kids getting into his things. His apartment was strictly off limits and he had little difficulty in keeping us out for it was scary in there. It took a lot of courage to go in, even to borrow something. To enter without a good excuse or an invitation was unthinkable. His windows were so dirty the rooms were dark as night even in daytime. He never swept much, made his bed, dusted or moved anything for it would have disturbed the mementos from his many travels. His whole life was displayed on tables and shelves and chairs and on the floor. He could sit there in the dim and savor all his past and he did not want it changed.

You never knew what you might find peeking out at you from some dark corner. Besides his ordinary sea shells and strange sponges, he had old dried things no longer identifiable, evil-looking plants from Florida, preserved specimens, baskets and boxes full of the unknown, and piles and piles of fearsome and absolutely fascinating trash.

It was all a grotesque, exciting jumble with everything displayed where it was handy to get out and show to visitors, to bring back sweet memories for Uncle Charles and for children never to touch.

A couple of blocks from our house, the Cumossette River ambled along one side of town. It was a never-ending delight and threat to us all. Down by Main Street, it had a dam that furnished power to run the water wheel in Herman Osler's flourmill. Usually the water rippled lazily over, exposing its broad and inviting top—great for wading across and daredevil showing off with boasting after, for drowning on the deep side above and getting knocked about on the rocks in the shallow side below.

Mother repeatedly told us hair-raising stories of fatalities on the river. Of George Meynar, who fell through the ice above the dam, and of handsome Blake Conover who was drowned trying to rescue him. She never failed to make it seem especially unfortunate that such a handsome fellow as Blake should have drowned so uselessly. And then there were endless reminders of the boy who "went over the dam and was never heard from again."

The river was our playground and every time we started for it she commanded us. "Don't go near the dam, you could be swept over. Stay away from the deep water above the dam." She never mentioned not wading across the top. Maybe it was just too much for her to contemplate.

Mother's admonitions never seemed to take the fun out of the river's delights, only to make the dangerous spots more appealing. Everyone's great goal was to walk across the river on top of the dam, splashing along smacking bare feet down through its inch or so of sparkling water and maybe stopping to do a bit of daring balance in the middle.

Anybody who did not have the necessary skill and courage—I did not—could go down by the mill and hang around and get to see someone who did, had waded over and lived. Then you could boast that you knew someone who had waded across. Some secret togetherness made us never reveal a name to any prying adult.

In a successful effort to save us from drowning, Uncle Charley built a big flat bottomed rowboat which would hold five kids, a dog or two, and assorted friends and their dogs.

All of whom could sit on one side without tipping it over. We took it down to the next street from our house which ended at the riverbank, launched it into the water, tied it to a friendly leaning willow tree and got ready to row away to Nutoon's Island and adventure. We all immediately sat on one side. The boat did not capsize so we dragged Gussie in from the water where he was swimming, pushed out from the bank and started upriver to study wild life, discuss the peculiarities of adults and have picnics. We seldom set out for anywhere without food.

The water was calm and sluggish. The inhabitants of the river and its banks were intriguing and life seemed good. There were money bugs, water spiders, waterfowl, old submerged logs which we called deadheads, aquatic vegetation, fish, frogs, turtles on logs and dumps, delightful dumps.

"Pull over to the dump," Pewee often said, "so I can get some literature." He was about the most eager reader in the family.

It was no idle proposal. The dumps offered old magazines and art not usually found on our living room library table and tin cans to hold worms for bait.

Sometimes the dumps were a good place to fish. We fished casually and frequently and never went to the river without putting a string, a hook and a few worms in our overalls' pockets along with a good, sharp knife to cut a pole as needed. We never caught much. The technique of fishing interested us more.

At night, the boys went "bullheading" in the deep water under the bridge. They kept scraps of raw meat hidden from Mother beneath the back porch until it was pretty rotten and smelling really putrid. The bullheads seemed to like it that way as they bit very well.

I always wondered why bullheading was, on every occasion, a night activity, carried out in a secret, deep hole under the bridge and was strictly for boys. I never found out and suspicioned there must be more to it than catching fish. Although I shared almost everything with my brothers, there was a line between us over which I was not permitted to cross. I never was invited to go bullheading and did not have the courage to go alone.

Cleaning a bullhead was a completely unnerving experience. Just to pick it up, look into its fearsome, half-dead eyes as it threatened you with its stinging feelers required great bravery, skill and confidence and an advanced stage of hunger. No matter how dead a bullhead seemed to be, you could never be sure it would not wriggle to life when dunked into a pail of water pumped up cold from our well. A bullhead never lost its ferocity even after it had passed on and become stiff as a board.

Someone was forever coming up with a new and better way of bullhead-cleaning which would remove the inedible skin, the terrifying head and effortlessly reveal the delicious meat inside. The best and most acceptable method was to nail the black, slimy thing to the barn door, slit the skin here and there and pull it off with a pair of pliers. Everyone usually compensated for the unpleasant task saying, "They are *so* hard to catch (which I doubted) and clean but the meat is *the best* of any fish." All in all, it was just plain fun that offered a challenge and a chance to boast about another accomplishment.

Life was never dull after Uncle Charley made us the boat. We could always "go up the river" and row its quiet, cool, deep channels, look and listen, fish and eat and ponder the wonders of Creation. And whenever our activities kept us overlong, we had the salutary, ever ready excuse, "We were stuck on a deadhead."

Charley also fixed clocks, lots and lots of clocks. A good clock in those days not only kept time with reasonable accuracy, but also announced its passing on the hour and each quarter hour between. He managed to get all of them running very well, but never seemed to be able to get them together for announcing the passage of time. And in the evening's din of our collective fun while he played his fiddle, we could hear his clocks banging and chiming away, each one vying with the others as to what time it really was. They all seemed to be arguing.

One with a big, throaty "Bong" would start. A delicate "Bing" usually answered. Then before another big "Bong" came, a clear, sweet chime would interrupt. So it went until the "Bongs" faded back against the walls and one last and insistent "Ting" finished up as though it had been waiting to get in the last word.

We knew the order of our days by Uncle Charley's clocks: getting up, going to school and getting the family's work done. And all through the night they kept us company. The clocks gave us assurance that our days would pass in a pleasant routine. They told us, too, that Charley was there in his fascinating and fearsome apartment making things to keep us happy and secure.

ANCESTORS IN THE ATTIC

Monday, September 7.   Morning
crept in today under a heavy fog. It is cold. Summer is closing down. My early morning musings bring thoughts of how getting old, living alone and having no one to talk to keeps me from having the satisfaction of giving advice, warning against dangers and making pronouncements about future happenings in order to say in the end, "I told

you so."

But it is not worth it. I would become a dogmatic old woman whose conversation is more to be dreaded than welcomed. Old age does not guarantee me any prerogatives or responsibilities. I do not need to run the world. Only enjoy it. That is enough.

Dave and Em and Dan came for dinner last evening. They seemed to have a good time. Em said, "I like your old-fashioned dinner."

I must be getting old. It is the only way I know how to cook: roast chicken with mashed potatoes and gravy and biscuits, cole slaw and lemon pie. I thought the Twins would burst eating. They sat and visited and laughed and told old war stories. Dave was "in" about five years, Dan for six. That is a long time out of one's life. We are fortunate that time's passage lets them laugh about it now.

Us Kids have seen two World Wars and innumerable "conflicts." The First World War touched us only slightly where we were away out in the country on the Old Old Farm. The Second, almost destroyed the whole family as we waited for news of the Twins and Pewee, sent food packages, endured rationing, worried and waited and yearned for the end when the boys would come home. That war is still with us for the careers and lives which will never be mended.

Grandmother McNaught came from Germany when she was eighteen. Never mind that our three other grandparents were Scottish and English, one German progenitor made us a German family in World War I time. During the long farm evenings when work was done, Mother and Dad discussed how the town would "take us." Although our country life made us feel secure and far removed from it all, we realized we would be fighting our relatives over there, Uncle Wilhelm and his family and that the folks in Hollandsville knew it. The town cousins were "on the other side of the family" and so had no roots "across." For a time some of them occasionally reminded us of our heritage whenever they could use it to their advantage. But after a while things calmed down and we were pretty well accepted as members of the righteous, religious and patriotic.

When the news finally reached us that the American Army had encountered the Germans, the family gathered in the living room on the Old Old Farm to talk about what we should do. Father's sister, Aunt Cora from Florida, up for her annual visit to get us reorganized yet once again, made the decision, "I suppose we should not write to Cousin Phoebe anymore," she pontificated. It seemed a shame to quit. How can you disavow a relative because of a war? It was not possible.

We enjoyed and admired her letters which were models of meticulous scholarship. Written in two columns, one a German Version, the other, English, they looked as if they had been printed instead of written by hand and were one of the first things I ever tried to read. Even then, I recognized her ability while I puzzled over the beautiful script and admired my school teacher cousin who lived so far away.

The Folks stopped writing and we lost track of Phoebe and put away the German part of our family. We never heard, or tried to find out, what happened to Uncle Wilhelm and all the rest. Their part in our lives was gone. But family traditions and rituals remain. They are persistent and pop up now and then. We remember and are proud.

Although Grandmother McNaught lived in Montana with Aunt Myrtle and we never saw her much, her speech and manner lived on in us. Potato pancakes for breakfast, "*ja*" for "yes," dedication to duty and hard work, a deep caring for family history. Family portraits, carefully stored away along with an old German scrapbook full of valentines, ribbons and locks of hair from relatives long gone, kept us aware of our past. We felt a kinship with the Old Country and those people because we knew Grandmother and she had known them.

For a while the family worried if Father could be "called up" or not. Almost everyone agreed farmers would not be drafted. "They'll never call up Bert," Mother frequently said as though trying to build her hope.

And Cora would roll her big dark eyes, smile her enigmatic smile and knock Mother's hope down with, "Well, I don't know."

In spite of the war, it was not long before our life went on in the routine that followed the seasons of ploughing, sowing, reaping, canning, butchering, waiting the winter out and forever getting ready to repeat the cycle. Evenings in the yellow light of our oil lamp, Father sang about "When It's Over Over There" and "When The Boys Come Home" while Mother played accompaniment on the family piano Grandmother McNaught had given us when she gave up her music. The folks around town seemed to forget our background, except when Father brought it back as he sailed through Wagnerian pieces and all the old familiar songs in German. It was a busy life without much time to worry about a far-off war where the rest of the family lived. They were forgotten. Living demanded our immediate attention.

When we moved to the Old Farm to be near the school in Hollandsville, our past, vivid and detailed in the pictures and scrapbook, was carried with us and stored in the attic there. It was a rainy-day haven and a lesson in genealogy. Accessible through a little door just like Alice's that led into it from the Twins bedroom, it brought back our heritage and became a part of our being.

The door was behind the dresser which I early learned to move by lifting one end and pushing it out just enough to squeeze through. Moving obstructions blocking the realization of my desires never bothered me much. I figured anything I could move an inch could be moved another inch and so on. The trick lay in not giving up.

The attic had no floor but, with luck, one could sometimes find a small board to put across the joists then sit in a quiet reverie while looking through the scrapbook and getting acquainted with the family's past. The only admonition we received about the attic was, "Never step down between the joists. That is the dining room ceiling with the dining room table below." We never seemed to need to be told how to crawl through the attic. Like so much of our behavior on the farm, we just knew or invented it on the spot.

Grandmother's old German scrapbook was enormous and very durable. The covers of hard cardboard were made to last for generations and the heavy paper pages never dried or cracked. In it she had pasted all the happiness of the Old Days, all the things she never wanted to forget: unbelievably lovely valentines and picture postcards from family trips saved when a trip was worth remembering. The valentines were the most wondrous. When I carefully opened their layers of lace, beautiful ladies and handsome men popped up standing on balconies surrounded with flowers and picket fences while soaring birds stretched white wings overhead.

The ladies and gentlemen seemed perpetually happy and contented as they smiled at me. Somehow it was a personal message and I could imagine myself a part of their beautiful world. Valentines in those Old Times were more than a greeting, they were an invitation to join in a joyous celebration of true love and happiness. They were serious and designed with intent to bring delight.

The family portraits in their frames of gold and curlicues were stored there too. We knew them all and their stories. It was like looking in a mirror when we thought we recognized parts of ourselves: a nose, a high forehead, big ears. We spent hours wondering and finding out who we resembled and discovered who we were. Ancestors became real people.

Whenever we all sat for an evening talking over the family's past glories, Cora never failed to remark, "Well, there was one who was a duchess, you know." She always emphasized the "you know" as though she wanted to make sure we did not forget. Then she added, "And Grandmother was flower girl to the Empress when she came to town."

Great Grandmother Munger was my favorite relative. It was said she had lived in Hamburg during the time of the Kaiser. Her father was a school teacher there. We were made to understand this gave him considerable stature in Germany at a time when class structure was deeply regarded. It seemed Great Grandmother fell in love with a man "who ran a store" and was therefore below her social level and her father objected, violently if he was like the rest of the family, and forbade them to marry.

She must have been locked up at home for the old story recounted, "She tried to sneak out of the house one dark night, fell downstairs and almost scalped herself trying to elope." The story was particularly appealing because Mother told me, "You look just like Great Grandmother Munger." I imagined a part of my face in her picture and my determined disposition in her behavior. She afforded me lovely fantasies of trying to elope, falling downstairs and almost scalping myself, when I would get my own way, lots of sympathy and attention and the Man of My Dreams.

Crawling carefully along the joists in the dim light took me past Mother's and Father's old love letters and then on toward the really dark part of the attic where the spinning wheel stood beside the chimney. A few times I stopped and read some of the letters. They were pretty nice and very romantic, but it seemed to be an intrusion and I really did not want to know as much about my parents as about Great Grandmother. Their past was too close, not yet enhanced by beclouding mists of time and their letters made me slightly sick. They, too, had eloped—although Mother had not scalped herself. She was so cautious and precise Father must have had to stand anxiously waiting for their escape while Mother calmly got the last detail of herself and her wardrobe organized.

On past the letters we came to the spinning wheel. It was too dark and cramped for us to operate where it stood. Consequently, Us Kids often hauled it out into the bedroom and ran it like the wind sending its big wheel flying while we imagined ourselves pioneers spinning wool and flax. Mother had a little bit of linen made from flax grown and woven by some grandparent and decorated with red yarn also spun by a relative. Somehow that little scrap of cloth made all the pieces of the family's yesterdays fit together.

The attic was our personal and private museum. In it we pictured the characters in the old family yarns that were becoming more glorious with each telling. I am glad my parents preserved our history in the wondrous attic and shared the stories with us. Now I can repeat them to any little relative who will listen and be forgiving when one of them says, "Oh, I've heard that a hundred times."

I like to spill out the old yarns just to keep them alive. And, whenever I catch an unsuspecting ear, to make the most of the opportunity to repeat them and perhaps offer some words of advice and caution to young ones in the family who will never visit the now-forgotten attic that the attrition of the years has effaced.

A DAY DAY!

Tuesday, September 8.

Abeautiful blue and white day today with the sun out again. I got up before daylight to look out the back bedroom window at the stars. Almost went out to visit Bert and Adah in order to get a really good view. They would not think me crazy if I drove in at five in the morning to drink coffee and look into their wide, dark country sky.

This is a day to do great things like moving furniture, polishing silver, sewing and cleaning.

It is not a day to sit and write.

It is a day that conjures memories of clear, crisp, cold winter days. If today were in January, it would be at least zero. It is a day that makes me think I might become fond of winter. Perhaps, because it seems so far away.

Delightful fantasies drift through my mind. I dredge up some old dreams and aspirations, work them over and flush out a few still serviceable ones. A day like this fills me with ambition and my head with plans.

This is a Day Day!

But, as old age advances, such fantasies and plans always seem to include the rosy, tempting glow of procrastination and I am content to dream away their loveliness. In fact, I prefer to dream.

So much for today.

SEX EDUCATION

Wednesday, September 9. Another

beautiful day, only thirty-seven degrees out this morning. I shall have to get the plants in from the deck. We surely will have a quick freeze on one of these clear nights.

My days go by in a bright, contemplative drift. The relatives stop by with bits of news and gossip. They are keen obituary readers and tell me who has died, who is sick and about their general health. Much of my life comes to me through the doings of others—the family and the town. I become progressively more an observer of life than a participant.

Adah calls with news of their many offspring. With five children and all the grandchildren, there is always someone who is sick or out of work, in need of money, care and food, terminally ill, getting married or divorced. In spite of all her children's troubles, Adah remains calm and reasonable. Her days are busy, hard-working ones filled with house and garden, cooking, cleaning, shopping and visiting the sick and lonely. It carries her along.

In one way or another things will work out for the family. The sick will recover or find grace, the troubled solve their problems and us Old Folks who were once Us Kids can settle down to some content. Things evolve. The family finds nourishment in its members and perpetuates itself. It is a matter of endurance.

Mother and Father were survivors. As they became older, they ignored problems, just kept on serving coffee and cookies and good food to everyone who came along. If no one came, they invited somebody. Like Bert and Adah, they had a routine of house and garden, cooking, cleaning, shopping and socializing. It kept them occupied and quite happy.

Years ago the family had about the same bundle of troubles as now. Each generation repeats the others. But, as I look back, disease and accidents seem to have been more fun than trouble and unbelievably exciting. We could not turn anyone over to hospitals and health insurance, but had to make do in the middle of war, depression and poverty.

Illnesses presented a challenge to which Mother and Father rose in grandeur and with great expertise, the result of much practice. Us Kids usually all got sick at the same time. Summer was throwing-up time, green apple stomachache, and always the predictable difficulties resulting from too many overripe fruits consumed along with quantities of dirt. In the winter we had measles, mumps, chicken pox, whooping cough, strep throat and flu. One of the most feared, scarlet fever, came in early spring. With no immunizations and no antibiotics, we were kept busy building our own immunity. It was fervently hoped we would "get everything hard enough so we wouldn't get it again." That was immunity.

Being sick was a time of special treatment. Our always-available practical nurse, Mrs. Evarts (whom we called "Aunty" effectively appealing to her sense of duty, obligation and love) came, Grandmother Dorset helped out with hard work and advice and Father boiled our best chicken or piece of beef to make us broth which he brought to our beds, hot and steaming with little pieces of homemade bread floating on its top. Mother shut off the front parlor for a sick room, got out the army cots (one for each child) and set out the slop jars and pans for spitting up in. Being sick with no plumbing was a messy business. But we got ice cream and attention. It was great fun and games for days on end. The sicker we were, the better, for then we "wouldn't get it again" and the attention and the spoiling would last longer.

Scarlet fever was the most dangerous and so the most exciting. I managed to get it twice on successive springs. Everyone agreed that "she didn't have it hard enough the first time." Isolation was about the only thing that could be done. No one wanted more than one child down with it at a time. It was believed that it maimed and killed and left warped minds. Whoever had it was put away in the parlor with the big doors barricaded so no one could pass through but Mother. Beyond them she wore a homemade gauze mask and a big blue apron. She was in control and in her element.

We were not permitted to leave the parlor for four weeks which allowed time for breaking out with the rash, treating the rash, which had little to do with scarlet fever therapy, and "peeling." In order to build an immunity, it was necessary to have it hard enough so you "peeled." If you were not so sick that you peeled, you would likely get it again. It was rather like acquiring a good sunburn, but with no sun: you turned red, peeled and itched but "no scratching." To give relief, Mother used baking soda paste spread on to dry to a crust which only made you itch more. It did afford some distraction though, for you could spend endless, fascinating hours cracking it off.

Peeling was the big thing. The morning I could announce, "I'm peeling! Look, I'm peeling!" I felt I had really accomplished something, could settle down to surreptitious scratching, would be getting well and be released from the parlor as soon as all my dead skin was off. Everyone was sure that the little flecks of skin would spread the disease so isolation lasted until we were done peeling.

It is to Mother's credit that she managed to keep us happy while confined for a month in the parlor, heated with a tiny sheetmetal wood stove and "stuffy" with little air. She permitted no windows to be opened for a draft was dangerous. No one explained why drafts were bad. Probably because they had been bad for generations. Even after peeling we were allowed outdoors for only a short time when the weather was warm and the wind calm.

Mother was forever feeling for swollen glands. She pressed her gentle warm fingers under your chin, peered into your eyes and ears and announced, "You have swollen glands," which was always followed by "Stay out of drafts." She could feel under chins on a clear July day and find swollen glands in a perfectly healthy child, which she treated with goose grease melted in hot turpentine and rubbed on chests and throats. Then she covered the application with a hot wool flannel cloth warmed on top of the stove or around the chimney of an oil lamp. If your skin held out and you stayed out of drafts you eventually got well, could escape from the treatment and get outdoors to play.

When Mother discovered I had swollen glands along with my second case of scarlet fever, she did some serious research in current periodicals and found the latest and most effective treatment was to "paint the throat and neck with iodine." So, no goose grease and turpentine for me. I was painted from chin to chest every day with the evil smelling liquid. There was some discussion about a new product called Iodex, a salve sticky enough to stay in place wherever it was applied which alleviated the need to mess around with the poisonous iodine. But Mother put her faith in the tried and true original odorous liquid and continued the treatment.

Iodine in those days was the real stuff. It burned like sixty in a cut and almost as painfully on whole skin. It was deadly poison and marked with a leering skull and crossbones. Mother repeatedly reminded us, "If you see a skull and crossbones on something, don't touch it!" To make sure, she stuck pins through the cork to keep us from pulling it out.

Iodine also was thought to be effective in preventing goiter. Every morning she gave us a few drops mixed in a glass of water. She got out the vicious bottle, shook in a reasonable number of drops then beat a tattoo on it while chanting, "Come get your iodine! Come get your iodine, early in the morning!" We dutifully lined up and drank it, poison or not.

After a few days of painting my swollen glands with no washing in between, my throat began to look like cracked clay which had dried under the summer sun. But my glands were "going down" so Mother kept up the applications every day.

"Mum, mumm," she ruminated while she examined my throat and felt my glands. "My, my they certainly are better." She felt encouraged and kept on, the iodine-soaked cotton swab making a scratchy sound on my scaly skin as she scrubbed up and down. Mother was never known to give up.

Not until my glands had almost disappeared did she stop the daily treatment. By then my skin was like old brown leather and peeling off in little hard flakes resembling corns. The iodine probably had little to do with my disappearing glands, but for the rest of my isolation, I was so busy picking burned skin off my throat, I hardly noticed, or minded, the slow passage of time. I did not get scarlet fever again.

The obvious drawbacks of our isolation would make it seem unbearable except that it became great fun. It was the caring that kept us contented. Mother never missed a chance to "feed our minds" so it was a wonderful time for reading, playing games and listening to her stories about "When I Was Little" and "Up North."

Michigan is the only state I know where Up North is a very special place and "Going Up North" is a very special reason for taking a trip. Up North clears your mind, airs your soul and fills your lungs with crisp, pine-scented air. Up North is any place beyond Clare and on up through the woods and wilds across the Straits toward the Sault. Along the way, you can glimpse beauteous, orange Tahquamenon Falls just before you get to Paradise on Lake Superior where Whitefish Point beckons to our friendly neighbor, The Dominion of Canada. Then still farther on through the pines, the great Keweenaw Peninsula reaches out another greeting toward the Canadians. Through all the years of the State's habitation, Up North has been a place of adventure, excitement and joy where one can hunt and fish, ski and skate, collect tall tales for repeating, meet interesting, bigger-than-life folks and just sit and look and look and never tire of looking.

Mother was fortunate enough to have lived there when the lumbering and settling commenced and the tall tales were aborning. Some of her best stories were about the lumber-camps and towns where she taught school in a one-room schoolhouse. In spite of forest fires, and with no equipment but a few books and her great imagination, she managed to instruct everyone who came along. I think she was able to teach the rudiments of reading, writing and ciphering well enough, but her greatest accomplishment may have been to persuade those wilderness kids to forsake their magnificent outdoors and remain in a ramshackle school-house to study and to learn. I think she made school there in the woods under the roughest conditions as exciting and fun-filled as she later made our scarlet fever isolation in the old parlor.

She told us about the days when forest fires filled her classroom with smoke and she and the students "could hardly see." She dared not send the children home through the woods into possible fire and had to have them all lie down on the floor and cover their faces with wet rags so they could breathe until it was safe to leave. Mother very probably used the forest fires to make education more fun than it would have been without them.

Smoke intrigued us. We imagined ourselves lying on the schoolroom floor, breathing through wet rags with the air too dense for study. We were no strangers to the bad effects of smoke but it was also great fun. We had exciting times of Leaf Burning, Junk Burning, Burning off a Weedy Field and, more than an occasional, Barn Burning.

Leaf Burning after dark presented many possibilities for a wild and thrilling time. It gave rise to the game of Running Through the Smoke which developed our ability to hold our breath for long periods of time. It added to our dexterity and sense of direction as we squinted our eyes tight shut in order to run far enough to escape the stinging fumes. Then we had Running Through the Smoke Two Times (for the very skilled, Three Times), Jumping Over the Fire (for the very brave) and of brandishing burning sticks to make circles and funny patterns against the night. When the fire was dying, we whacked it with sticks to make sparks fly. We made our own fireworks and had them anytime we could find something to burn. It made a forest fire with smoke seem a delightful occasion.

While Up North, Mother lived above the drugstore owned by Aunt Geneva and her husband, The Doctor. All the folks around came there for anything and everything both day and night. She told of Saturday nights when racial prejudice was still rampant and Old Indian Pete got drunk and slept on the front doorstep of the store, making her have to step over him to get inside.

From the story, we learned that sordid things of life do

exist, and that they can be overcome. I imagined Mother in a lovely long dress, probably white, trying to step over Old Indian Pete and wondered how she ever got her skirts over him without tripping. I did not wish to criticize her but felt sorry for Old Pete and thought someone should have covered him up. Her lesson seemed to be, "Do whatever the occasion calls for in the best way you can. Sometimes the best thing to do is to ignore it."

I wondered what Mother was doing out so late at night in that wild country but later discovered she and Father were secretly courting and she had to come home alone. There were many old family tales and smiles of how "Albert was often seen in the early morning coming out of the back living quarters of the store carrying his shoes." It was from the North she and Father eloped by train to be married in Canada and began to produce Us Kids.

The yarns went on, always exciting, always teaching. She never failed to point out the need for resourcefulness, efficiency and bravery. It was a little strange for she was lethargic and indifferent to the harsh demands of life on the farm. Time, The Depression and the care of Five husky kids had worn her down. Perhaps she wanted to remember the days when she had been ingenious and had the time and opportunity to innovate.

Mother was often in the store alone while Aunt Geneva did her housework and Doctor drove his horse and buggy out into the lumber camps to care for the sick and injured. It was one of those times when they were both away that the Sliver Story originated and Mother again demonstrated her ability to contrive. Wood slivers and splinters around the camps were sharp as needles and could be as long as a sword. They caused hideous injuries and even killed as they shot from the lumbering and milling machinery.

"One day a logger came into the store with his mouth

open making an unintelligible noise like 'Arugh! Arugh!'"
Mother's tired voice began as she recalled those vigorous
times. It brightened until she sounded as if the story had
happened only the day before.

"I couldn't tell what was the matter with him and he
couldn't tell me," she went on. "So I pulled him into the
light from the front window and looked in his mouth and
down his throat to see what the trouble was. Every time he
went 'Arugh!' I could see a big sliver almost as long as a
clothespin jumping up and down whenever he tried to talk.

"I sat him down and got a pair of tweezers from Doctor's
office and had him open his mouth. But each time I reached
in, he gagged so that his tongue got in the way."

By this time, several of us were experimenting with a
few trial "Arugh Arughs" and gagging to see what happened to our tongues as we lived the story with her.

"So," she casually told us, "I took him back into the office, got a towel and told him to stick his tongue out. As
soon as he did, I grabbed it with the towel, held on and
pulled out the sliver."

When Mother stated these facts, she was making sure
that, should any of us ever have to remove something from
a throat, we would know exactly how to do it. The story was
another lesson in self-sufficiency. That was why she told it.

She told us about two loggers who got in a fight so
fierce one chewed the other's ear almost off. Mother did not
fix that one, Doctor did. Sometimes the North defied even
Mother's innovation. But, whatever the problems of the injured and sick, they usually ended up at the store where
some sort of healing and a measure of understanding might
be obtained. There was no other place to go.

Mother used a North Woods happening to introduce me
to the seamy side of life—the dangers of sex. I had always
suspicioned there probably was a seamy side. A sense of sin

must be ingrained as part of our original mental equipment. So, to let me know that sex could have undesirable consequences, even dangerous ones, she told me about the woman who performed an abortion on herself with a piece of rusty fence-wire. I really did not know what an abortion was and she did not explain. As usual, not wanting to reveal my ignorance, I just waited for the story to evolve, feeling sure things would become clear in due course. It did and made my preadolescent insides all squinch up when she said, "The woman went out into a field, broke a piece of rusty wire off a fence, rammed it into her insides, aborted and died."

Unpleasant as it was, I grew up knowing about pregnancies and abortions and acquired a healthy regard for septicemia, the dangers of fooling around with the natural order of things and, of course, getting pregnant in the first place.

To me, the whole lesson of The Woman Story seemed to emphasize the desirability of proper surgical procedures much more than the dangers to body and soul of sex. In my imaginings, the threat of rusty wires overshadowed the perils of pregnancy and possible abortion. And I wondered why the woman did not use a clean wire. Wicked or not, she would have been alive which seemed a somewhat better outcome.

For years, I pictured the whole of Up North covered with rusty fences and almost forgot the lesson about ill-considered procreation. Perhaps Mother emphasized the wrong thing.

She persisted in her object lessons with a story about a woman who had her husband assisting her with a difficult birth. In his eagerness to help, he had reached into her to pull out whatever he could grasp, had misjudged and pulled her bladder out along with the child. Being resourceful as well as alone in the wilds, he simply sorted out the baby and stuffed the bladder back in. By the time Doctor got there, there was not much of anything left for him to do.

Mother's stories were certainly entertaining and fascinating, though not always pleasant. But life is not always pleasant and she intended I should understand it and that, with a clear head and resourcefulness, even the most unbelievably difficult problems could be solved. She did not emphasize the sordid and lurid nor did she embellish or make specious the truth. She told it like it was and never covered up anything. She taught us to believe in ourselves and gave us hope and confidence that, in spite of great difficulties, we could endure.

GOD HAS ONE EYE

Friday, September 11.   P_{ap and}
polyp checkup time. I dread it—waiting for pathology reports, hoping for the best, yet fearing the worst. Two years of apprehension have been hard to bear.

I wonder if getting old means slowly falling apart. Of every morning, and often in the night, checking to see what part of me has deteriorated. Perhaps time on my hands makes me more aware of any dysfunction and increases my self-concern. There need to be busy hard-working times during old age to make enjoyable the happy, loafing ones. Life should make one tired then "Rest In Peace" can really mean something.

Summer work on the farm made resting times thoroughly enjoyable. Resting time was Sunday. It was called "A Day of Rest" anticipated with joy but often proving to be a day of compete boredom, restrictive Sunday clothing and inactivity.

Sunday was a day for going to church, eating a lot, visits from the relatives and sitting around eavesdropping on adult conversation in order to pick up the latest family gossip and for playing What Can We Do Now?" If Mother did not come up with something fast, we invented something which tended to get our Sunday best covered with grass stains, dirt and manure.

Getting all five of us ready for church was serious business for Father and brought all his meticulousness. He attended to our grooming. Mother scrubbed faces, ears, knees and sometimes feet. We got washed in only the dirty places. She used a washbasin which held about a quart of water and the same washrag for us all. Usually the water was cold and made us shiver. Sometimes she warmed it up with a little from the teakettle and made us feel really clean.

After the scrubbing, Father lined us up, combed hair, polished shoes and urged, "Now, stand up straight with your toes pointing straight ahead." He was a fiend about these things, particularly about slicked-down hair as against having it stand on end. He frequently cut off the tops of Mother's old silk-stockings, tied one end in a knot to make a cap and attempted to get the boys to wear them at night to keep their hair from getting rumpled while they squirmed in their deep little-boy sleep.

My toes somehow never pointed straight ahead or even in the same direction. Father knew I was proud and self conscious about trying to remain a feminine girl among four brothers. "You walk like a duck," he said and pointed to my feet in ridicule. Then he demonstrated, waddling along to shame me.

I tried to please him. But it was many years, until I had acquired some heels and went dancing before my toes pointed straight in front of me, my feet became dainty, I fell in love with the Prince in Cinderella and someone admired my feet. Then, my toes pointed as they should and I did not walk like a duck.

Mother often tried to ease my hurt pride by telling me, "Ballet dancers walk like ducks." It took some of the cloud away, interested me in ballet, and gave me a reason to be myself as I dreamed of footlights and fancy, fluffy costumes. The ballet was a long way from us where we were out there on the Old Farm. I wonder where Mother got her information or if she made it up.

Father's attention to personal appearance sometimes impelled him to employ cruel persuasion. As summer faded into fall and on toward the winter Holidays when our church going would stop until Easter, his efforts turned from persuasion to force and he became completely dedicated to making his wild and wooly tribe into a well-groomed family for at least one day a week.

Pewee was a very stubborn Kid. He rebelled against silk-stocking caps and hair-combing and refused to cooperate.

"Brush your hair," Father commanded one Sunday morning forcing the brush into Pewee's hand and wrapping his fingers around the handle. Pewee resisted and stood motionless.

Father yelled, "Brush your hair." Pewee stood stock-still, straight and immovable.

After a few more tries, Father stretched Pewee over his lap and applied the hairbrush.

Corporal punishment was unusual in our house. Bert and I were terrified as we watched, certain that Father would give Pewee some permanent injury. We screamed and wept. Father whacked and yelled, "Brush your hair," and Pewee just lay stiff and still across Father's lap and took it in silence.

In a futile effort at persuasion, Father pleaded, "Brush your hair down—just once!"

Pewee refused. Bertie and I kept up the din and Mother, unable to endure the commotion any longer, thrust us out the back door into the cold woodshed and lifted us into the coalbin where we were trapped. So we yelled still louder in a vain effort to be heard in order to protect Pewee who was standing up for all of our rights by protesting too much grooming.

As we were shut in the coalbin outside, I never knew how Pewee and Father came out. Probably Mother interceded or Father got tired. Church lost its luster after that and we did not go so frequently anymore. I think Father gave up on our Sunday "spiffing up" although he continued to chide me for walking like a duck. I know he always wanted the best for us. I doubt he knew how to get it.

After the fiasco of Sunday grooming, Father became as determined to provide us with more than adequate food as he had been to keep us well-groomed and Sundays became days of eating and eating. We almost always had chicken, a live one that came from the chicken yard and was in the pot in less than two hours. It had to be caught (always exciting), picked (always nauseating), dressed (always an anatomy lesson) and cooked. Father never failed to take time to teach us everything he could about food preparation. None of us were ever to grow up unable to produce our own food and to enjoy doing it. In his way, he continued to demonstrate his deep concern for our welfare.

Then, as forever after, Sunday meant chicken dinner. As soon as the boys and Gussie had managed to capture and kill and Mother and Grandmother had picked, Father got ready to cut up. His work was exquisitely meticulous and so predictable it developed into an early Sunday morning ritual beginning when he grabbed the naked, picked chicken by the legs and smacked it down on its back on the kitchen table where it lay supine, its yellow feet sticking up in the air fairly asking to be eviscerated and severed limb from limb.

In order to make sure I learned how to do it, he had me stand on tiptoe peeking over the edge of the table where I watched and wondered at Father's dexterity while he lectured me on the precise method of making a dead chicken into delicious Sunday dinner.

First, he carefully cut off the wings while he explained to me how the joints worked for flapping and occasionally flying over fences. He set them aside, patted them and said, "See? Isn't that nice?" He liked his meat to look good even when raw.

Then, he cut off the legs through the joints next to the body and separated the thighs from the drumsticks, he patted some more and explained about bone structure. He showed me the difference between the wing joints for flying over the chicken yard fence and leg joints for walking and added "ball-and-socket" and "hinged" to my growing vocabulary.

Next came the tricky part of separating the "front" back (the upper back) from the "back" back (the lower back) from the breast. With surgical precision, he cut through the ribs and removed the breast. By feeling, he could find the place between the two halves of the breast to cut it into two pieces. Next, he separated the back back from the insides. (No one ever said "guts" in those days.) More patting before he put all the parts in a pan with baking soda water for scrubbing. We had very clean chickens.

The insides remained on the table gleaming deeply red, greenish and purple. He carefully pulled the intestines away from the gizzard and the liver while explaining, "Never cut the liver so you leave any green gall on it."

"See that?" he asked pointing with the end of the knife. "That's gall. If you use any of that it will turn the whole chicken bitter." I grew up with a great respect for gall.

I did not get sick as Father slit open the gizzard and emptied out its fetid contents, only hungrier. He opened the sack of partially digested, evil-smelling chicken food and, pointing again with the knife, turned the contents over to separate the little stones from the rest.

"See?" he went on. "There is the grit the chicken uses to grind up its food. Without that, it couldn't digest anything. That's wheat and oats and grit and grass." And he pointed out all the aspects of chicken digestion.

It was an exciting and sad time whenever we inadvertently cut into a "layer" and discovered eggs among the entrails. Once in a while, we found a white-shelled, completely-formed one lying shimmering in the eggsac waiting to be delivered for breakfast. And underneath, several more undeveloped eggs without shells resembling solid, golden yolks. Then tucked deep down in the chicken's insides, a cluster of little, just-forming eggs that looked like yellow and orange beads.

While I watched Father cut up the Sunday chicken, my knowledge increased and I waited anxiously to grow tall enough to stand over the kitchen table and be able to do it myself. His enthusiasm and pride in the job taught me how a chicken was put together and of how it got to be a good eating chicken or a "layer," of how it lived and how it died.

Some things were forbidden on Sunday. Playing cards and sewing were the major ones. There was some question about knitting. I never saw anyone knit on Sunday. In those days sin was carefully defined. It was comforting. People really knew where they stood. Cousin Beata was said to have sewed on Sunday. I always imagined her being forced to mend a rip or sew on a button. And that she only did it to keep her beautiful clothes on. In her case, it did not seem a sin.

I admired Cousin Beata and usually found an out-of-the-way place to sit where I could watch her while she visited on a Sunday afternoon. Mother must have noticed my green-eyed, greedy-gut staring at her magnificent wardrobe and tried to offer me condolence and an explanation by telling me, "Cousin Beata buys her clothes on sale at the end of the season and saves them 'till the next year."

I knew there was never any money, in season or out, for snappy things for me. I always got the hand-me-downs. So I watched and planned to grow up to be as lovely as she, inherit her clothes and sew on Sunday when it was absolutely necessary.

When relatives came to visit, they filled the idle hours boasting about their children and grandchildren and gossiping about the sinners in the family. Cousin Pearl was about the biggest sinner of all. She hennaed her hair and "lived in sin" with a great hulk of a man who was a rich contractor. She was beautiful, self-confident and wore expensive clothes which she bought during the season with lots of the contractor's money and did not look as if her sins weighed very heavily upon her.

Cousin Pearl had a Pekingese dog who could say, "Ma Ma," play hide-and-seek and was the same color as her hair. I always wondered if she dyed the dog too. When she and the contractor came to visit, the Folks let me stay to watch the dog tricks, then they pushed me outdoors saying, "You go outside now, dear and play so the grownups can talk." I was certain it was to keep me from exposure to her wanton ways, knew all about the arrangement, did not much care about who was sinning and grew up convinced that all contractors were big hulks and quite inclined to sin. It seemed pretty much all right to me. They were happy, rich and absolutely fascinating.

Sundays were the days when the good was sorted from the bad. We were supposed to "clean up and behave" and eat and eat and eat. Perhaps the Folks thought they could keep us out of mischief by continuous feeding.

Mother tried to control our Sunday behavior by cautioning us, "God can always see you." It gave me a terrible feeling of guilt whenever I strayed and of being protected when I was in trouble. Mostly, I went my carefree way imagining God's great eye in the sky watching me all the time and winking now and then. Often, I could see Him smile.

Probably not queer I imagined God with only one eye.

RELATIVE COMPETITION

Monday, September 21.   I think we take the measure of our lives from the lives of those around us. We feel taller, shorter, more or less talented, slower, older, more or less capable in terms of the capacities of others. We make excuses for what we deem to be shortcomings and seek the reason for our existence in relation to those who touch our lives.

We do not have Sunday dinners and visits anymore as in those old days that kept everyone in touch with everyone else. Advancing age insulates me and brings fewer and fewer people near enough for me to make comparisons. People once so near have moved off into their own lives and, as they have gone, they have taken a part of my life with them. I am diminished by their departure.

When there is no one left to furnish us a measure, we

are alone and old. Staying young seems to be a matter of keeping enough friends and enemies around to enable comparisons. Measuring one's self with one's self during the ending of life is dull and destroys contemplation of the future and satisfaction with the past.

Grandmother Dorset spent a lot of time comparing how I measured up with other folks and made a great effort to "keep up," which meant clean and neat, curled and combed, wearing dresses and with no manure on my shoes. It was impossible to avoid manure there on the farm. We had paths and a few boards here and there to walk on to get to the chicken coop, the W. C. and the front door of the barn but cement walks were unheard of.

Being the only female child in the house, I was Grandmother's primary target. She had a little pocket-size hairbrush with a Celluloid handle from which she was almost never separated. Whenever I got within her reach, she straightened my clothes, brushed down my hair, gave me a push toward the kitchen sink and said, "There now, go wash your face and hands and neck and ears."

If she couldn't reach me, she captured me. "Henny, come here and let me brush down your hair," she commanded as she whipped out the brush and I would have to submit.

My hair was straight as a string and slippery. No hair ribbon had ever kept it in place. Grandmother seemed to think she could force it down on my skull by pounding on my head with every downward stroke of the brush. It made me dizzy and, as soon as my head quit ringing, I plotted my revenge and eventual escape.

Whenever prim, proper and beautiful Cousin Beata came to visit, Grandmother never failed to go into a flurry of hair brushing and cleaning. I really longed to grow up to look like Beata, but never cared to leave off my hoyden life in order to achieve it. Grandmother's ministrations convinced me looking like Cousin Beata would take a lot of crimping and curling and washing and pressing—and a lot of time. There was not that much room in my busy day. Whenever work was done, the outdoors beckoned and I escaped to enjoy life rather than to conform to the constricts of society.

Grandmother's penchant for cleaning up must have been triggered by her intense desire to demonstrate that, in spite of primitive farm life, I could be fit competition for the Town Cousins. Whenever she and The Aunts got together, she wanted more than life itself to be able to boast about me. Being able to clean a chicken, split wood, slop the hogs, climb and swing and run like the wind did not count. Such mundane accomplishments did not show. But she could brush my hair, straighten my dress, exhibit me before the assemblage and smirk with pride. I didn't have to do anything—just stand there and suffer. I knew it was absolutely stupid because I could never come out ahead. The Town Cousins felt themselves superior and that was all they needed to make me a loser in the family competition.

After automobiles and improved roads came along to bring more relatives out into the country more frequently to our door, the competition really intensified. I hated every minute of it and hated the Town Cousins too. It made us perpetual enemies. We never did "get along." We fought like fiends and everyone wondered why.

When the Sunday afternoon inspection in the living room was finished, I usually took the Town Cousins "out back" to show them how to swing from the ropes in the barn, jump in the hay mow and, as a special treat, offered to take them to secret places to pet new kittens and little pigs and to hold wriggly new lambs. Maybe even to watch a chicken lay an egg if we could catch one at it. And when there had been butchering, to inspect the entrails that had been thrown out into the back field. The heads were often there too and the Cousins were visibly impressed. I could plan they would retch and run at the sight and smell of what had been a cow or a pig and now lay spread out on the ground in the hot sun. All but Cousin Maxwell. He never let it be known that anything could get the better of him.

After a trip "out back," to see the wonders and realities of farm life, The Cousins were wrinkled, sweaty and, most likely, had stepped in manure. (I counted on their never remembering to watch where they stepped.) When we got in I was the accused aggressor and the Town Cousins the suffering victims.

After the Relatives had gathered up their progeny and left, Grandmother said in despair, "They are such nice children. Henny, why do you treat them that way?"

And my Sunday afternoon would end much as it had begun before anybody had come to visit: comfortable and peaceful, dirty and free, wild and rumpled. No matter that Grandmother felt certain she had lost the battle of conformity to the town's ideas of proper dress and behavior, I always felt that, in the end, when I took things into my own hands, I had won.

But Grandmother was fair. She never asked anything of anyone she didn't demand of herself. She never neglected her clothes and her person and she was infernally modest. So far as I could tell, she had been born with her clothes on. We shared the same room but I never saw her even partially naked. She had a fetish about nakedness and only spoke the word in a hoarse whisper as if it was worse than a cuss word.

I always wondered what she wore "underneath" but never found out. No matter how early I woke in the morning, Grandmother was up. Before I ever opened my eyes, I could hear her snapping her snaps and scraping her hooks as she rustled into her clothes.

Counting out from whatever was underneath, she put on: ruffled under-drawers, a corset (stiff as a board), corset cover, petticoat, blouse and skirt. And in winter, on top of it all, a fascinator around her shoulders for extra warmth. At the last, she pinned a dustcap on her head. She said it was to keep stray hairs from falling into the food while she cooked. Grandmother most surely never got cold and she was always clean because she never got dirty.

Often, in early morning, she waked me muttering and clucking to herself as she sorted through the clothes I had taken off the night before. She held each piece up in the early morning light next to the window and went through the same ceremony with each one, "Tch, Tch, my Oh my." She gave each garment a shake or two, laid it carefully on a chair, smoothed out the previous day's wrinkles, patted it a little, moved on to the next one and said loud enough so she was sure it would wake me, "Is this all you wear? You'll catch your death in no more than this."

She was "set in her way" and never quit trying to get me into proper clothing and to make me into a little lady fit for the competition. I think she realized it was a losing struggle. But she kept on trying even though she knew times were changing and long underwear and petticoats were gone forever. And that I never in my life would wear a corset or a dustcap.

She never quite believed that existence was possible without layers and layers of clothing. I will always remember her hurrying around the house, busy with her work and looking as if she was a whole closet full of clothes on the move—not quite a person—and with a Celluloid hairbrush in her apron pocket. Grandmother's proper clothes, cleanliness and neatness were like her perfect spelling. It put her indelibly on the right side of the social order: neat and clean and a good speller. She was sure it was everything needed to make a good life.

ICE STORMS

Monday, September 28. This is a day for contemplating winter and the changing season. A cold white frost last night makes winter seem a real possibility. I remember many past mornings: cold ones, stormy ones, hot summer ones when the heat left over from the day before pinned us down. Stormy winter mornings were our favorites for they brought weather that offered interesting things to do as they promised more and more snow and ice for skating, skiing and just wallowing in the soft, white stuff. Grandmother Dorset called it "wallering" and said it with a wicked, threatening sneer, "Now, if you Kids go wallering in the snow, you sweep off before you come in."

Sweeping off was part of the fun of wallering for it gave us a chance to land a few well-directed, lively blows on each other while we wielded the porch broom. For some reason, known to children and never remembered by adults, pummeling one another on any pretext, short of actual combat, is great fun. Grandmother never really understood the seriousness of rollicking roughhouse. She was all for accomplishments like good grooming and continuous hard work.

Whenever ice storms came to bedazzle us with their beauty and threaten us with their icy power, we forgot about wallering and spent the day watching and waiting, filled with awe and a little afraid that our lives could never be the same again. On those days a fine rain started in early morning, then, as the day wore on, the temperature dropped to stop suddenly at the freezing point. Instead of the rain turning to snow, it kept coming down to freeze on grass and trees and bushes and buildings. All day long we watched through our steamy windows while ice built up on everything. After while, the branches on the front yard pines bent until they touched the ground, making them look like icy green tents. We knew pines would not break but waited and listened for the crash of falling hardwoods and learned about the resiliency of different kinds of wood.

The day passed with all of us looking out from inside as we stayed glued to the windows watching and speculating on how long the raining and freezing would last and if it would turn to snow. Either prospect was a delightful and exciting contemplation while we planned on going out to enjoy whatever the storm had brought us as soon as "it let up."

The whole farm came to a standstill, waiting. By afternoon, a sheet of ice covered everything. It got so dark, night chores had to be done in the middle of the day: warm water carried down our slippery paths to the chickens and hot swill to the pigs for we knew it would be very cold before morning.

Mother lighted the lamps while it was still daytime and all evening, after chores were done, we sat huddled close to the coal stove listening to the storm. The rain rattled against our windows, the front yard pines moaned beneath the weight of their branches and the whole world seemed frozen in time. When night came, the wind rose and we could hear the crackling of ice on the trees when it broke loose and fell with a clatter on the hard ground. The hardwoods down in the swamp creaked and cried as if in pain. It was like listening to our most favorites die when their branches broke off and fell.

"There goes one," someone said. And we all kept still waiting.

After a very loud crack, "That was a whole tree," somebody else announced with expert conviction.

Then, "That was another one!"

We all listened, quiet and afraid, fascinated and awed, reverent at the power of the rain and the wind and ice. With the sun in the morning, all outdoors shone in rejoicing that the storm was over. It was time then for skating anywhere and everywhere. We skated to school right down the middle of the road. Or we all got on Murning's bobsled and slid down into the valley almost all the way to school with never a thought of having to climb the hills to home. We just wandered back in the late afternoon stopping to slide up and down on the way to hot cocoa, night chores and warm fires.

Days of ice storms were the most thrilling and terrifying of all the days of winter. It was the terror they brought that made them so great and so much fun.

SCHOOL!

Wednesday, September 30. The dark

hangs outside the windows this morning, not as the absence of light but as a presence in itself. Rain comes down, thick as syrup and sticks as though about to freeze on. It slants in cold from the west and blows on the deck wetting everything still out there: the picnic and plant things, paints and pots and a few pieces of furniture. Fall rains are the wettest of the whole year.

This is a cold, worry time—a time to shun or to ignore. It hauls unpleasant thoughts into my mind and brings out old, dilapidated worries that should have been thrown away long ago. But, in spite of everything, there is much to keep me busy and fall has its attractions. It provokes anticipation of winter's beauty, hope for spring and gives meaning to summer's passing.

Each season makes the next one an intriguing expectation and the one that is past, a cherished memory. We are fortunate to be able to remember the good and to believe the future will be better. Lasting memories are woven from the bright spots of the past, as well as rousing old yarns and plausible tall tales.

That is the way it is with the Now. It could never be enjoyed if there were no past and no future. Now is the time between. It doesn't last long, which is a blessing. If Now were forever, we would have no reason for hoping and nothing to reminisce.

I used to worry about the time between the past and the future, the time we call Now, and the place that must exist between one thing and another. Walking home from school past Herman Osler's flour mill and on toward the Cumosette River bridge, I kept my thoughts on the place where my feet touched the sidewalk and speculated that there must be such a Place where the bottom of the soles of my shoes and the top surface of the sidewalk came together.

Neither could be part of the other. The top of the sidewalk could not be a part of my shoes and my shoes could not be part of the sidewalk. They each had to be entirely separate. So, there must be a Place which was neither sidewalk nor shoe.

But, what was in the Place? If it was a place, it probably was filled with something. Maybe I just sort of floated along above the sidewalk never really touching it at all!

It bothered me intensely. But kept my mind busy and made the trip past the mill, over the bridge, through the Park and up the hill on the dusty road to home, a walk of enthralling conjecture. Sometimes my ponderous thoughts bothered me, but I never told anyone about the Place, nor ever asked some wise adults whether it could exist. I was sure they would not understand—or even listen.

After Halloween passed and the cold settled in, the cracks in the sidewalk were mercifully obscured by snow and ice and school became as much a battle of wits with the elements as with the absorption of facts. The days were wet and cold. We had no slickers and no boots for the mile walk to school. When our family finances permitted, my brothers had "arctics" to pull over their shoes and fleece-lined coats ordered from the Sears Roebuck Catalogue. Sometimes I borrowed one of the coats and relished its warmth wondering why I could not have one. But unisex clothes were unknown then and all winter long I was forced to shiver in propriety in a skirt with only black sateen bloomers underneath.

Mother dressed me in proper girl clothes. My coat usually was one that would look good sometime in the future— far in the future—for I did not grow into things as expected. The pockets never got above the level of my knees and I had to bend over almost double to reach into their depths to retrieve the few cents I had salvaged from the grocery change to buy candy. Having to run the errands had some compensation, but frequently resulted in severe stomach cramps after I had hungrily munched my ill-gotten sweets.

My coats were "good wool" and scratched. They were stiff and drafty. The warm air escaped out around my collar to let the cold rush in around the hem. It shivered up my legs, to be heated by my skinny body before it escaped out the top to draw more cold in at the bottom. In those coats, I was a walking convection current.

But the winter trudge home from school was not too uncomfortable. I watched the snow-covered cracks in the sidewalk pass beneath my feet and figured the snow must be filling The Place where my shoe soles met the walk. My mind was freed to wander and wonder, to think about the coming Holidays and the next day of school.

Mr. Quinten, our janitor, made the cold days warm and toasty in the classrooms and kept us busy and contented in our spare time at noon and recess. He held a special place in the staff hierarchy and in our hearts. Not just a janitor, he was The Janitor. His staff classification was discrete. He related to no one else. "Ask Mr. Quinten," was the standard reply to anyone seeking permission to get in, get out, use up or replace. He was the supreme source of special privilege for students, teachers and even for administrators. Mr. Quinten ran the school and we all knew it.

All the teachers disappeared at noon leaving, by some informal agreement, all of our fun, mischief and discipline to Mr. Quinten. He controlled us by keeping us happy, for he made it more fun to be good than to be bad. If we dared mischief, a word or a glance from him was enough. He never threatened us with what he would do if we broke his rules. And, not knowing, we dreaded what it might be. He never gave us a chance to balance off the odds against getting caught. He had power and he knew how to use it. It derived from the things he let us do, not from what he prohibited. No teacher or student ever questioned Mr. Quinten simply because life at school would have been unbearable without him and surely would have been less fun.

On rainy or cold noonhours he let us play Hide-and-Seek in the big basement storeroom. It was long and narrow and dark. The only light filtered in from the door so the farther back we scrambled, the darker and more delightful it became. Just feeling our way along was an adventure as we climbed over big cartons of toilet paper and chalk, extra dustrags and soap. The storeroom had a good smell and assured us we would not be wanting for the necessities which made school life comfortable.

After the cold walk to school, we escaped teacher supervision by ducking down the back stairs and going to the furnace room where we could leave our mittens to dry and get warm while chatting with Mr. Quinten. As we stood around him waiting for school to start, he took out his big pocket watch, snapped it open and told us how long it would be before he "Rang the Bell," which made us feel secure and gave us an inside track on avoiding tardiness.

There was a rope in the basement hall which reached up through two stories to the big bell in the little coop on top of the building. He was careful to ring the bell long enough to give us time to get to our rooms, then he pulled the gong when we were supposed to be in our seats ready to work.

That gong was the knell of fun and the beginning of learning. Every morning and after each noonhour, we raced the gong. To be out of your seat when it twanged was a serious infraction and meant long hours after school to atone for a few seconds delay. Somehow, Mr. Quinten managed to delay pulling the gong until he was sure even the slow ones were able to get in and sit down.

The furnace room was our refuge and a haven of peace. We didn't need to do anything there. Only sit and soak up the warmth of the furnace and Mr. Quinten's understanding and get fortified to face another day of education. He kept us warm, entertained and encouraged.

We knew we could go to Mr. Quinten with whatever went wrong. He fixed broken shoelaces and arctic buckles, replaced lost buttons with safety pins and filled up the hungry ones who had forgotten their lunches. He understood when teachers did not, he took time for us when teachers hurried off. He was calm, deliberate, efficient and eternally dependable. The teachers knew it and we never had any difficulty getting permission to "go see Mr. Quinten." He solved as many problems for the staff as he did for us. Every school and every child should have a Mr. Quinten.

We ate our lunch in the basement dining room where the caste structure of our school life dictated where each of us would sit and where we would put our lunch pails. The little kids, The Twins, sat at the near end at the little, low table, the grades sat in the middle at the middle-sized table and the big kids at the far, exclusive, isolated end at the big table. (The School Board surely must have read *The Three Bears* and taken it to heart.)

Lunch pails went on a shelf against the wall beside each particular table. Our lunch for the five of us was packed in one large, two-layer pail, which made problems. The chicken sandwiches, boiled eggs and salt and pepper papers had to be parceled out. While I was parceling out, it seemed reasonable for me to sit at the little kids' table with the Twins so I could peel their eggs, do a bit of mothering and avoid having to make any decisions about where I was supposed to sit.

After while I belonged at the little kids' table and there was no place for me with the grades. I never did make it to the big kids' table. By the time I was old enough to consider it, we had moved to town to keep Uncle Charley company and all went home for lunch.

The whole lunchroom arrangement became just another step in my never-ending battle with convention and conformity.

October

NO SANTA CLAUS?

Friday, October 2.
A cold east wind roused the sun up this morning and reminded me that the fall chores are still not finished. I have brought the plants in from the deck and hung them on poles beside the big glass door in the living room to wait until spring. Now, there is nothing left but the barbecue cooker, the plant potting things and my cherished wind chime. It sounds like a ship's bell ringing and clinking driving away loneliness and making me feel warm and cared for.

The deck is one of the great joys of living here. It makes the place seem more like a house than an apartment. Because of the deck, it is home. It is a place for drinking early morning coffee and bird-watching, handicrafts and flower-arranging and letting clutter collect until I can spend a lovely, lazy day in the sun straightening and reorganizing while I make plans to sit out there and dream. It is like a porch.

A porch gives shelter. In the days when people walked

or drove horses a quick storm brought all sorts of interesting folks "up onto the porch": peddlers and tramps and travelers, neighbors hurrying home ahead of the weather and young folks "out sparking."

Mother liked to tell about how people used to get caught in storms and "not being able to go any farther, drove straight up into the front yard, tied their horses to a tree and rushed up on the porch to wait out the storm."

Often, I can imagine hopefully, the storm lasted a long time and whoever was waiting on the porch was invited to stay for supper. Mother made these seem the happiest of times when people enjoyed people and even passing strangers could spend a festive evening eating with the family, swapping yarns and waiting for the weather to change. Porches are an invitation to some of life's greatest delights.

This first cold makes me think about Christmas and I have been making many lists. Christmas Day often seems a let down after all the frantic shopping and preparation. Not so with Us Kids on the Old Old Farm. We had snow and sleigh bells and Santa and mountains of food. Our Christmases were truly storybook, unbelievably perfect with no plumbing or central heating to detract from the rustic luxury of the day.

Monstrous packages filled with all the goodies which make childhood bearable began to arrive early in November, coming by rural free delivery from every corner of the country. Oranges, kumquats and grapefruit came from Aunt Cora in Florida; big red bananas to fry, guava jelly and lovely embroidered nightgowns from Cousin Effie in Puerto Rico. From cold Montana, Grandmother McNaught sent us the leggins, mittens and caps she had knitted to keep us warm. And toys: beautiful, wonderful, intriguing, brightly colored toys that told us how much the relatives loved us and how well they understood what Christmas is all about. There were wheels that really turned to propel something somewhere, things that buzzed and rattled and hummed, bells that really rang, drums and horns and, sometimes, a play fiddle. All of it fragile and guaranteed to break before the fascination wore off and none of it durable enough to destroy bright dreams of future acquisitions.

Mother hid all the packages at the far end of a long, narrow closet that ran beside the upstairs hall. It was the only one in that big house on the Old Old Farm. The front was filled with the clothes we were currently wearing. The back received the discarded ones. Things were just shoved along as they obsolesced so the farther we went into its dark recesses, the further we traveled into the family's history. Nothing was ever thrown away, it was "put into the closet" from which things emerged as "new" garments, "made-over" garments and, finally, as rags for washing, wiping, scrubbing, nose-blowing and for stuffing in cracks to keep out the cold.

No one much ever went to the farthest depths of the closet—there was no need to go there except at Christmas. Mother put the colossal boxes as far back as she could and then just kept shoving as more arrived. By the first days of December, it became too much to endure and I began to explore the prospects for receiving with complete disregard for the blessedness of giving. After all, the relatives could not be blessed if no one received.

It was dark in the closet. We had no electricity for lights and I can never remember a flashlight in the house. I had to feel my way along pushing against clothes hanging along the wall and stacks of old shoes piled on the floor. But after a time, things began to take shape as I scrunched myself against one side so as not to block the light coming in through the door. Navigating the closet to assay Christmas required a high degree of stealth, skill and much practice but the rewards were always worth it.

The mails then were about like they are now—damaging. So the boxes arrived with a few rips and loosened string which enable me to slide the string, enlarge a rip, feel around inside and package-pinch until I got hold of something which felt interesting and could wriggle it through the rip. Finally, if it seemed to be worth the risk, I took the package to the front of the closet for closer inspection. Apprehension for my sin was improbable, for all the adults in the house had more important things to do than chase kids out of closets full of Christmas. Nevertheless, I was careful to replace the wrappings, confident no one would notice.

As Christmas came nearer, the rips got larger, I had a well-worn path cleared past the old clothes and shoes and had a pretty fair idea of what we would be getting. Few gifts were addressed to anyone of us in particular. They were just wonderful things to make Christmas glorious fun for us all.

After the groping and ripping and guessing, I remember only one present that really thrilled me: an orange plastic pinwheel airplane on a stick. When I blew on it, it whirled around like the very dickens with a deliciously satisfying rattle. I blew on it for hours, there in the closet, watching it spin until I worried it might be worn out by Christmas and my package-snooping deduced by some clever grownup.

At last, the big night would come. When Father and Less Lawrence had cut the tree out of our woods, forced it to stand upright in a bucket of dirt and sat it in the parlor, it was Mother's special responsibility to see to the decorations. As always, she gave attention to our developing minds, encouraged us to help and demonstrated exactly how to do it.

The decorations came from Grandmother McNaught's collection of crystal baubles to which we added strings of popcorn. And, at the very last, carefully fastened little metal clamps holding real candles to the tips of some of the branches. To make sure the tree was brightly lighted but still would not burn up along with the house, required detailed planning, a lot of skill and experience and pails and pails of water set within easy reach.

"Fasten the candles where there aren't any branches above them," Mother cautioned as she hunted for little limbs that stuck out and were strong enough to support the weight of a lighted candle. Somehow, the danger of fire added to the excitement and the apprehension only increased our joy.

No candles were ever lighted until it was time for Santa to come, all red and white, laughing and stomping his black boots as he bent under the huge pack on his back. I, fortunately, was spared the shame of seeing the, by now, dog-eared and bedraggled packages brought down and put under the tree where everyone would be able to remark about the condition of their wrappings. They mysteriously ended up in Santa's pack and were distributed when he came. I never wondered how the things got from the closet into his pack. That was Santa's business and part of Christmas.

On the great night, after supper was finished and the dark wrapped us in the mystique of the Holiday, the tension of waiting was almost impossible to stand. Mother and Father and Grandmother gathered us together to sit on the floor around the tree and carefully put a pail of water between each of us for "putting it out." The candles were lighted and we began to wait for Santa.

When we heard sleigh bells, stomping on the porch and "Ho, Ho, Ho!" the Folks cocked their heads to listen, as though they thought we couldn't hear and slyly asked, "I wonder who that is?" as if we didn't know.

Santa, all snow with the big pack on his back, came in,

bowing and "Ho, Ho, Ho-ing" and asking if we had been good. There was noise and laughter and many questions about our past behavior and not many answers. We sat silently and waited, certain that confession is neither good for the soul nor the better part of valor. Especially at Christmas, it is downright stupid. Sometimes I had a few guilty thoughts about my many trips to the back of the closet but they were soon forgotten as the ripping and tearing open of packages was about to become acceptable behavior.

Santa gave out the gifts and, as we rent their wrappings tossing the paper aside, Mother stood at the ready to fling pails of water in case the tree, along with the family, should catch fire. We might have been drowned, but we surely never would have burned up.

Somehow the "goodness" of Christmas was always judged by the depth of the paper and string on the floor. Invariably, someone would say, "Just look at that pile of paper," never, "Just look at those presents."

It was not until I was almost eight, and we were about to move to the farm on the hill above Hollandsville so I could go to school, that I began to wonder, and found out the facts, about Santa Claus. I always turned to sophisticated Cousin Maxwell who lived in town and was my senior by two years, for answers to life's ever-recurring perplexities. Whenever there was something important to talk over, we went to the front edge of the lawn well out of earshot of meddling adults, sat on the grass, dangled our feet in the ditch and discussed things such as relatives, how to get to an inside bathroom at school and what it would be like living in town.

It was during one of these times when, on a warm summer day, Maxwell broke the news to me about Santa. He had been telling me about how things would be after we moved when he said, "Living in town where there are other kids is really a lot of fun." Then he gave me his most serious and superior look and broke the news about Santa. I think he was hoping to make me well informed so he would not be embarrassed by the naiveté of a country cousin and he wanted to cover all the important things a first grader should know.

"That Santa Claus," he volunteered, "that's really Uncle Charley."

I was shocked. I had never quite believed all the North Pole stuff but liked to think of it as a possibility and hated to have my dream shattered. To cover my surprise and grief, I said airily, "Yeah, I always knew it." I did not want to be patronized by Cousin Maxwell or to admit that I had held on to the dream until such an advanced age.

Even then it made me realize time was passing, that I had to grow up and go to school and that dreams had best be clung to, no matter how many folks tell you differently.

Christmas still means snow and sleigh bells to me with combustible trees proffering real candles, heaps of paper and pails and pails of water. Christmas is still Uncle Charley. I'll always believe and hear "Ho, Ho, Ho," when the dark comes on the magic night. He made my dreams real with his love for us all and his caring. And by sharing his own dreams. I think he believed in Santa Clause too. He must have in order to have played the part so well.

THE DARK PARK

Saturday, October 10.   Took the

car to the garage before sunrise this morning. The walk back home in the early cold let me participate in the starting of a new day. I stopped under a hickory tree and picked up a few nuts to take to brother Dave's country place for planting. At age sixty-two, he is busy raising trees, fully confident he will see them mature and fruit.

A black walnut stands a few feet from the hickory. The squirrels are eating the hickory nuts and do not touch the walnuts. I never would have thought about their diet had I not been walking. Not that it is very important, but it is always nice to have an extra bit of information with which to confound an unsuspecting listener.

Before cars and garage repairs, we walked for pleasure, for getting places and for noticing things. It was excellent for exercise and education and gave us a keen awareness of the weather and of the seasons. We got acquainted with the neighbors and the strangers we met. We knew just how long it took to get places. No being held up by bus schedules and traffic. We were on our own.

We found out about the shortest distance from here to there, and to somewhere, and learned geometry by "cutting crosslots." We could cut crosslots and shorten the walk to school by two blocks if we went through, instead of around the Park. The Park was something that had to be conquered with its real and imagined dangers, and yet to be enjoyed with its beckoning, serene beauty and blandishments. It was a festal gathering place and a battleground where muscle and imagination were needed to contend in order to achieve social stature.

Lying about halfway between the Old Farm on the hill

and Hollandsville with the school in the valley, its two hilly, green acres were the demarcation between the customs and traditions of country and town. It had trees and paths and a bandstand for Fourth of July celebrations, two wading pools full of soggy, dead leaves and bugs, a lot of slippery moss and a little water. No self-respecting frogs ever used the pools for croaking and splashing but the town and country kids splashed and soaked there in oblivious abandon.

The Park and its pools were cool and inviting on hot, summer days with the dead leaves and slime invisible beneath the surface. And all the kids who had bathing suits wallowed blissfully there in the foot or so of water. Not so with me. Many times I was forced to pass the inviting, cool shimmers as I walked back and forth on summer trips for groceries and supplies from town. Tired and sweaty and burdened with bags of necessities, I was tempted, but no bathing suit meant no cool dip.

Finally, one very hot, summer afternoon, I made up my mind to disregard the lack of proper attire and enjoy the enticement of the Park pools. I got into an old dress and underpants and set out down the dusty road the half-mile to the Park. I was pretty warm by the time I got there and wanted to jump right in. But plunging in fully clothed seemed imprudent and to demand an explanation. I considered pretending that I had fallen in and vaguely wondered if maybe I couldn't bait one of the kids to push me in. I stood on the edge of the pool a while curling my toes over its cement rim, teetering back and forth, debating various courses of action. Nothing feasible came to mind so I stood for a few minutes pretending to watch the kids who were swimming and finally in desperation, threw caution to the winds and jumped in hoping no one would notice I had my clothes on.

"Look at Henny! She's got her clothes on!" all the kids yelled out. I was not sure if they were admiring my bravado or making fun of me. I ignored them and splashed about, did a few belly flops and crawled around letting my body float out behind while I pushed my way along "walking" my hands on the slimy bottom.

No one played with me and I pretended not to care. I actually felt a certain élan and derring-do about jumping in fully clothed. At least I had not had to fuss around getting into a bathing suit as they all did—just jumped in as I was. It made me feel very good about myself and very independent.

Afterward, the walk back home down the dusty road in my sopping condition presented more problems. I had contemplated bringing extra things and changing in the Park privy but could imagine no adequate explanation for Mother's or Grandmother's demanding query, "Henny, where are you going with all those clothes?"

Some of the kids changed in the privy but it was dirty and full of bugs. A quick gallop home seemed the best and most convenient solution except that I was uncertain as to how I might be able to explain my dripping wet rush down the dry, dusty road. Society is always demanding explanations.

Trying to find a way to appear socially acceptable, I decided to take along an old umbrella and planned to tell any nosey, solicitous adult who might inquire about my soaking wetness, "Oh, I got caught in the rain."

So with great aplomb and complete confidence in the plausibility of my story, I scooted down the road in the bright afternoon sunshine, my explanation in my head and the old umbrella as evidence of a violent, and very local, thundershower. I met no one and was vaguely disappointed. It had seemed a good yarn. And I wondered if it might not have worked.

By the time I got home, I was completely dried off.

Having no more need of the umbrella, and being faced with providing another explanation as to why I was carrying it on a clear day, I quietly stashed it in the umbrella stand beside the front door and sauntered through the house. No one noticed. No one cared. I was elated at having defied the "bathing suit for bathing" tradition and began to think social mandate might be overcome quite successfully.

After accomplishing a trip through the Park, we came to the sidewalk. "Getting to the sidewalk" was anticipated with joy and relief. It meant easy walking with no dusty road and hills to climb. Besides, we felt very elegant and "citified" as we scuffed our leather-soled school shoes and clumped along on its hard, smooth surface. The sidewalk made us real city kids and we felt sure that, once there, our country ways would not be so evident.

Being from the country always put us a little beneath the kids in town. It may have been because our living there was not a matter of choice but of necessity. We had to work at raising our food and felt inferior to the town kids whose folks bought everything at Morganheiser's Grocery, Thebald's Dry Goods and Knute's General.

The Park with the river at the bottom of its hill was our triumph and our defeat. We slid there in the winter, envied the kids who swam in the wading pools in summer, danced the Maypole dance in the spring (under duress), celebrated the Fourth of July, were hounded by the Big Kids who chased and teased us the year around and romanced there when we grew older. Walking its woody, root-tangled path on the way to school was frightening for me. Sometimes, when I was alone, cowardice took over and I "went around by the road." The Park path was a challenge not always met. But after its hills and trees and dark depths were conquered, I could scurry across the bridge, get on the sidewalk and feel safe and victorious.

The threat of the Park was very real. Its cone-like hill bordering the path offered shelter for the Big Boys who hid there while they pelted us with small stones as we sauntered along affecting a great show of confidence and bravery. Whenever the stones came thumping down around us, I stopped and listened then inquired of my brothers, "Did you hear that?"

They never paid much attention and casually replied, "Uh Uh," and went on kicking at roots and leaves and thinking sad, lonely, going-to-school thoughts. Either they knew where the rocks came from or, more likely, did not care and looked forward to becoming Big Boys to hide and harass from behind the hill. I felt responsible for my brothers and worried when we left the sunshine of the road and climbed the cement steps to start down the dark path. I knew someone was raining stones on us and not being able to see who it was made it more fearsome.

Scaring little kids in those days seemed a legitimate sport for big kids. It was usually Sam and Jasper Kroul who bothered us the most and often waited on the bridge like trolls to waylay us on our way back and forth. They picked on us as a duo and we lumped them together in fear and derision as the "Kroul Boys" or the "Krouls."

One day Jasper picked up Bertie and, leaning across the iron railing of the bridge, held him out over the water. I felt powerless to help and had to stand there terrified, remembering that Bertie could not swim. The water looked deep and the drop very far down. I was not sure the Kroul kid could hold on to Bert and knew that if he lost his grip, the fall to the water would surely be the end of my brother.

Bertie, as always, acted prudently. He never wiggled a muscle or cried a bit but hung there limp as a rag while Jasper taunted him about not being able to swim and dive and kept jiggling him up and down. Finally, he stood Bertie back on the bridge and we ran toward the Park path and home. I hated and feared the Kroul boys all my life and when they had some remorse and tried to make amends, I was reluctant to believe them.

They had a pony they frequently rode to school in a great show of affluence and horsemanship. I hardly dared look at them whenever they trotted grandly along past me. One day, on the way home, as I was leaving the safety of the sidewalk to enter the dark Park beyond, Jasper came along on the pony, pulled up beside me on the bridge and asked, "Want a ride?"

I stopped and scuffed and looked at the ground not daring to go on my way, imagining that, if I did, he would pursue me, grab me and throw me in the river. I thought about screaming but did not for I had my pride and had aged enough to feel a tinge of romance in the situation.

I kept on scuffing, looking at the ground and stalled for time. I had long since discovered it was a good way to get out of difficult situations and felt it looked quite pathetic and evoked a lot of sympathy. At a later age, scuffing helped me to get my hips swinging so I could walk away as if not really caring.

Jasper coaxed. I scuffed and, at last, submitted. He hauled me up, set me in front of him on the pony and took me all the way home, clear past his house and on up the hill to the Old Farm. On the way, I began to realize he was a boy and I was a girl. That he held his arm around me protectively and was almost kind. But old suspicions overcame beginning sex and my heart stayed in my mouth every step of the way.

I should have mistrusted the Krouls less after that, but never did and always expected them to pop up from behind a hill with a handful of rocks to throw at us or to come galloping along on their pony to overtake us and do us damage. Nothing ever lessened my qualms about the Kroul boys and the Park.

Besides being the site for our acculturation, the Park was a natural location for the town's gravity fed water supply. On top of its steep hill overlooking the river, a big, black standpipe let untreated river water down to us. It was never for drinking, only for washing and flushing. There was not one sign in the whole town: "Unfit for Drinking." Everybody was expected to know it.

When late fall days turned to winter cold and we were older, the Park became our playground. The sliding route down the steep standpipe hill challenged us with its humps and bumps and trees that grew crowded close together. If we started at the top with a good fast run and belly flopped, we could get up enough speed for the sled to fly into the air when it hit the humps and come slamming down only to climb the next one and crash down again on toward the stone steps of the gate that led toward the sidewalk and the river where we were forced to stop. To avoid the steps we slued around and slid down a little bank. If we missed the turn and "took the steps" we were sure to be thrown against the cement gateposts.

I usually made it to slue around, go down the bank and managed to stop before getting to the river. Once in a while I missed, hit the abutting gateposts and went limping home with assorted bruises. When Mother quizzed me, "Henny, why are you limping?" I concealed the hobble in my step and recovered to slide again the next day. My reputation as the only girl who belly flopped down the steep hill required that I show up every day to prove that I could do it and to keep in practice.

During all of our going-to-school days, The Park was our mentor. It gave us joy and despair, made us courageous and crafty, scared us with its darkness and soothed us in its cool shade. Its snowy hills developed muscles few athletic programs ever could have offered. It was the locale of our social development. Our walks through the Park accomplished our journey into maturity.

The steep standpipe hill still looks inviting when I pass it on trips back home. And the sledding scars on its snowy sides invite me to come back and ride them one more time.

FLIES, FIVE FOR A PENNY

Monday, October 12. The television is fixed after a fashion. It makes everyone look as though they have very short legs and no chins. Changes in the angle of the picture give quite astonishing results, almost more interesting than if the set were "well adjusted." I fear its days are numbered. Meanwhile the distortion is surely intriguing.

Went to church then to Dave's little farm yesterday. He and Emily plan a visit to their son next week and I shall be chicken-sitting again. Often it is a little confusing for me to remember if I am out there to keep the flock alive for egg laying or to help butcher them.

The chickens probably have cost Dave about seventy-five dollars each what with building a coop, fencing a yard and researching chicken care. But they have given him that much fun and recreation. So I will chicken-sit a few more times until they all land in the freezer.

I would miss them if they were all lying stiff, cut up and frozen, their engaging chicken personalities lost forever and turned into prosaic edibility as broiled, baked or fried. A cooked chicken is not as interesting as a live, clucking, squawking, crowing or cackling one, as sex and chicken culture may dictate.

Chicken-sitting is a lovely quiet time. I carry water and mash, gather eggs, round up a few wayward ones that escape as I open doors and gates. And always, I must be on guard against The Old Bastard and Frankie, the two reigning roosters of the flock. After a few times sitting there, I have learned never to turn my back on either one. They strut around waiting for a fight and give no warning before going into a flurry of feathers to hit me somewhere about my head and shoulders.

Perhaps their macho instincts are triggered by Adeline, the eternal mother. Addie is a good layer, but as soon as she has popped out a few eggs, she begins to cluck and settles on her nest to "set" and begins to raise a chick or two. Frankie and the Old Bastard keep her protected and pregnant. She never fails to have a good hatch.

In the peaceful evening there at Dave's, the country sounds and smells fill the air: the soughing of the wind in the pine grove, some rustlings in the grass, and rattles of weeds, fall crows cawing overhead, geese go honking along, a far-off train toots as though lonely and looking for a friend. Now and then a deer crosses the yard stepping along in no hurry looking content and secure. A few well-fed neighborhood dogs go by marking their territories leaving spoor on all their favorite spots.

It is a good time, chicken-sitting: going out in the frosty early morning to carry feed and water and in the quiet evening, listening to the sounds of the coming night as I make things secure against predators with a taste for poultry. I come in through the greenhouse and the studio to a pleasant evening of aloneness to dream old lady dreams and mull over some of my more treasured memories: the coming of fall coolness and chickens and chores on the farm when we were still all together, my brothers and I.

We looked forward to the fall and the cold after a good freeze with a sense of relief for it meant the end of Fly Time. Our years were divided not so much by the seasons as by what we did. There was Gardening Time, Canning Time, Butchering Time, Planting, Weeding, Cultivating, Haying— every activity had its time. We parceled the parts of our years by the names of the things we needed to do.

Fly Time was one of the more exciting times, besides Butchering Time which was hard to beat. Fly Time overlapped all the other Times from early May when the first flies crawled out from their hiding places in the warm spots of the house, the barn, the pigpen and the chicken coops, to the first good frost in fall when we hoped the last one would freeze to death.

As sure as the spring sun came to heat up the manure pile behind the barn, they started to hatch and by hot weather invaded the house in swarms, evidently preferring the food inside to anything they found in the barn, the pigpen and chicken coop. We fought flies all summer long and looked forward to fall when they would all be gone.

The flies were nasty and made us itch when they crawled about on our skin, but really did not do much harm except for the dirt and germs we believed them to carry. Grandmother was very positive about it and announced with her usual sniff, "Flies carry germs." And that was that. She and Mother were deeply concerned with germs. They scrubbed and scalded, scoured and scraped and "shooed" in a never-ending battle to protect us from the diseases they bore.

Mealtime was the most expeditious time for shooing flies. It took special equipment and great organization to get a meal on the table before the flies could light on the food, cover it with germs and make it inedible. We never suffered the dangers of insecticides. Our only defense against flies was swatting and shooing. When there were too many to swat, we shooed.

Shooing required several Fly Swishers which Mother made by using a piece of old broomstick for the handle and a large paper flour sack she fringed for the Swisher. Our flour came in twenty-five pound sacks, just the right size for an effective Swisher and we wore out many brooms so we had plenty handles. She folded the sack several times and slashed strips part way up it to form a fringe, leaving enough at one end to wrap around the broomstick to be tacked on forming a sort of early day pom-pom. When grasped firmly by the handle and moved briskly, it rattled and swished and shoed the flies—hopefully out the door.

As soon as it was about time to set the table, some adult, usually Mother, commandeered a child and got ready to shoo flies. The adult was to do the shooing and the child, to open the screen door quickly enough to let the swarm of flies out but not so soon as to let any more in. We knew we were really grown up when we got to shoo. Then Mother or Grandmother said, "Go shoo the flies while I get the meal on." It gave me an opportunity to gain great stature when I was permitted to shoo and could order someone younger, "Get ready to get the door while I shoo."

Mother was our best shooer and attacked the chore with great zeal and dedication. She went at it as though the flies with their load of germs were an invading horde about to decimate her family and she, the only one who could save us. While Grandmother worked over the stove at the far end of our kitchen dining room, Mother went to stand at the ready in a corner, raised her arms over her head and, holding the Swishers high, prepared to make a pass across the room and over the table swishing and shooing and driving the flies in a great black, buzzing swarm toward the door where a child was stationed.

"Get by the door! Get by the door!" she commanded.

"Now . . . Get Ready . . ." The frenzy was unbelievably intense. Mother swishing and shooing and calling orders, the flies zooming frantically ahead of her and everything depending on the child at the door who was supposed to crash it open at just the right time. If you were the door-opener, you had to bend almost double to scrooch low enough so as not to obstruct the passage of the cloud of flies racing in a swivet ahead of Mother as she rattled the Swishers.

Just before the black buzzing cloud hit your face, Mother shrieked, "Open the door! Open the door!" Then quickly, "Shut the door! Shut the door!" In this way more flies went out than came back in.

After a successful pass, she sighed and smiled encouragingly. The child holding the door felt important at having done a job well and Mother went back to the corner of the room to make another try. When I was the door-opener, before I got old enough to shoo, I always sort of hated to see fall come to freeze the flies. Mother made me feel so needed, efficient and important. She knew how to make almost everything exciting and fun.

By the time Grandmother had the food on, the room was pretty clear of flies except for a few stragglers which were taken care of by a child appointed to keep them away from the meal by waving a flyswatter above the table, just clearing but never touching anything. It was a real challenge to come close to the food without hitting it. However, with practice, and we got lots of practice from May to the first good freeze, we developed considerable dexterity.

Standing there shooing, surveying and smelling the deliciousness was torture for a hungry young stomach. But with a little care, it was possible to keep the swatter clear of the table and grab a surreptitious sample while Mother and Grandmother were still busy at the stove.

I was frequently tempted to swat a persistent straggler or two that landed on the table. The crack of the swatter coming down always brought out the familiar order, "Don't swat flies on the table. They carry germs." Sometimes Grandmother added, "They've crawled around in the W. C. and carry germs," which really emphasized the point.

It certainly followed that the alternative was to let the flies crawl around on the food for a while, then squash them flat. This bothered me. Why not swat them in the first place before they could spread dirt and germs all over? But no one listened to any of my suggestions and I was never permitted to swat flies on the table no matter how logical it seemed.

After meals and before the next one, Us Kids swatted and collected flies. We got a penny for five. The money was pretty good especially if we "salted" some good flat swatting spot with a bit of food. The flies would light there and could be smashed dead, easily and surely. Frequently, live flies stopped to nibble on a departed comrade, consequently, I never picked up dead ones until I was sure their attraction as fly food had diminished.

I found that flies tended to land on the same spot again and again. So I skipped around each room, swatted the available ones and, when I returned, others would be back squatting in the same place. It got to be a dance-and-swat routine. I practice a nice, full swing with a good follow-through like the tennis players I had read about in the *Saturday Evening Post*. While on my way around and around the room swatting and following-through, I was practicing tennis, developing dance steps and dreaming, not killing flies. Sometimes I got in a little backhand or a good volley along with fancy footwork. It added exuberance to my chore and made the swatting sound as if I was really dedicated. Sometimes, I swung at nothing at all just for practice.

Besides swatting and shooing, there was one other potent way to get rid of flies. We nailed a can with a little kerosene in its bottom to the end of a broomstick. On cool evenings, when the flies swarmed up to the warm ceiling, all I had to do was hold the can over a fly that, as soon as it sniffed the rank oil, lost its grip, fell into the can and drowned. Then all that remained was to fish out the carcass and claim money. Compared to the inefficient hot weather efforts of fly swatting, cold weather trapping made it a breeze. It made fly killing and counting the dead unbelievably easy and increased my profit astronomically.

At a penny for five, I made a fair income. If nothing else, it gave me a basis for dreaming about a secure financial future and of being able to buy candy at Knute's store, Christmas gifts for the whole family and seductive articles of clothing—maybe even a pair of rayon stockings. My dream of rayon stockings was always clouded by my worries about how to keep them up. But they seemed a good solid sexy idea and I dreamed on. My stockings, of whatever kind, had never stayed up anyway.

Swatting and shooing flies did not seem a drab or paltry chore. Mother's enthusiasm made it a great and exciting adventure and convinced me that it was a real worthwhile activity, necessary for preventing disease and assuring our survival.

It was not entirely the money.

NO MONEY

Wednesday, October 14.   Once
in a while a day comes along which might better be left out
of my life. Yesterday was that day for no special reason until
evening, when Amy came for supper and a visit. She, as
always, is incredible.

I was sitting in the car on the campus waiting to pick her
up when she came swinging along the sidewalk in her confident way, her red-gold hair flying and shining in the sun
as she hurried back from chemistry class. Amy walks as if
she takes great joy in moving through the air and feeling
the ground pass beneath her feet. And she carries no white
cane. She makes no false steps, never stumbles or asks directions. I cannot watch her and believe she is blind. Only
when she senses a curb or some stairs, does she stop to feel
with her toes then bounds on her way again.

I spoke to her as we met so she would know I was there.
We chatted on the way into the dorm. She held doors for me
and led us through the crowded lobby, never bumping into
anyone, up the stairs to the second floor, down the hall and
around several corners until we came to her room. We got
her errands together and set out to spend an evening
visiting, telling "blind" jokes and enjoying ourselves.

She is learning to handle her school money so we
started a bank account. "Put my finger on the line so I know
where to sign my name," she said. She located the line and,
using her left index finger to guide her right hand, she
wrote a meticulous "Amy McNaught" while explaining, "I
have trouble dotting the i's and crossing the t's." Numerals
are easy for her but she has no idea of how to spell the
amounts on a check and explained candidly, "I cannot
spell." She has never seen a word and Braille is written in

contractions. We had a brief conversation about how the sound of a word "says" the letters it contains, devised a few helps, and felt we had the business of banking and spelling pretty well conquered.

We cooked supper and visited into the quiet evening. She talked to me about her pride in never appearing blind and gleefully described how she fools people. Teachers are her prey. She lets them ask her to do things such as write on the chalkboard then says, "I can't. I can't write." After letting the teacher berate her, "What do you mean, you can't write?" she states, "I'm blind." It is her joke, the teacher's chagrin and the delight of her classmates.

She tells me, "People look at my eyes and think I am high. I just let them keep on for a while asking me what I'm high on, then tell them, 'My eyes are this way because I'm blind'." She expresses her contrition for the discomfort of others and says, "It's better than going around announcing to people, 'I'm blind' all the time."

Amy takes great pains to lead a normal, college-girl life, rushing, dating and dancing. "You just can't make it," she says, "unless you're socially well-adjusted. Some blind kids I know will never make it because they're not adjusted." She is serious about her education, gets excellent grades and plans to be a teacher.

Amy makes me certain that good-for-nothing days should not be waited out and wasted but instead, used exuberantly to enhance life.

For us on the Old Farm on the hill above Hollandsville, the Great Depression was a string of long days to be waited out and pushed back into the past, while we hoped for things to improve. Hope came hard then and Mother and Father must have believed our despair would never end. Without the farm to raise our food, I doubt we could have survived. There was no public assistance, only friends and relatives and they had little more than we. People made it on their own or not at all.

Father looked everywhere for work. He went to Detroit to stay with his sister and her husband, Aunt May and Uncle Fred. They wrote that he had collapsed one hot day as he trudged the streets with no streetcar money. No one seemed particularly concerned about his physical condition. It only furnished us with another family yarn to be added to the ones we repeated over again and again.

When Father came home for a visit, he told us how he had lain on the sidewalk and looked up into the eyes of strangers who were bending over him watching and staring. People had nothing else to do then but stand and stare. When he regained consciousness, he heard someone announce, "Here he comes." Then, he found himself slipping away and heard, "There he goes!"

No one called an ambulance. No one did much of anything but stare and wait to see if he made it. Crises were times to be waited out, not overcome. "After a while," Father said, "I got cooled off and rested up and went on." It seemed his collapse there on the sidewalk was the sum of the whole drama of the Depression. No one could do anything. Everyone had to wait and endure.

In the summers we lived on the farm so we could raise our food, letting Uncle Charley shift for himself in the big house in town. It took all of us working in the fields to grow and preserve enough to feed us until another summer and another crop. Plowing the garden was a problem because we had only Old Flory left of our team. The other half of the team, Nelle, (She never was called Old Nelle) had been shot as no good because she let Flory do all the work. Whenever Father slapped the reins across their sweaty, grey-white backs, Flory strained into the harness but Nelle just stood still and waited, forcing Flory to pull her along with the load. About all Nelle ever did was help a little to keep the whiffletree even.

I never was quite sure what made "them" shoot Nelle and suspicioned she must have done some terrible deed worse than balking by the wagon tongue. I eavesdropped on all kinds of adult conversations but never was able to find out. In spite of her obvious guilt, I admired Nelle. She was independent and not to be coerced into anything. She always got her own way. She was glamorous and a dilettante—also dead. Life was simple then. A useless farm animal could not be tolerated.

My most vivid memory of Nelle was the way she smelled after she had passed on. We were all back in the woods for a walk one day, Father, Mother and Us Kids. Going for walks was popular in those days since it cost no money. The woods were a welcome relief after the trek down the hot, sunny lane and across the soft dusty soil of the pickle field where we grew cucumbers to sell to the local pickle factory. Cool and inviting, it was our own personal playground and amusement park.

On this particular day, Us Kids galloped ahead investigating here and there, looking for small trees to pull down to the ground for jumping. Whenever we found a young green maple, we shinnied up, pulled its top down, grabbed hold, kicked ourselves up and the tree snapped us to the sky. It was wonderful going up, kicking and "flying," but difficult getting down. If our weight did not pull us back to earth, we had to climb down the trunk. But all the bother was worth the breathless leap and the thrill of feeling our insides still on earth as the rest of us flew up. I still have dreams of flying high through trees and looking back down to where I have been.

As we went through the woods exploring, climbing and "flying," we began to smell Nelle. Mother sniffed and asked,

"What is that smell, Bert?"

Father muttered and veered our course toward the outskirts of the woods and back to the bright sunshine of the pickle field. Now the woods became ominous. The more so when Mother inquired, "Did you bury her or leave her on top?"

Dad muttered again.

I suspected Nelle had been "lightly covered with leaves" like Hansel and Gretel and that she must be lying, rotting and stinking under one of the many woodland hummocks which are soft and squashy to step on. I could almost feel myself sinking through the leaves and getting stuck in Nelle's decomposition.

The smell seemed to diminish after we changed our course. "Well," Mother said, "it seems to be going away. Are we going away, Albert?" She always used his full name whenever she was insisting on an answer.

Dad did not even bother to mutter.

As we walked gingerly toward the bright sunlight, I could hardly wait to get out of the woods and step on the cultivated soil of the pickle field. No more tree jumping and climbing. The woods had changed because Nelle lay there.

I never enjoyed going back to those woods, much as I loved them with their trees to send me flying. From then on, I skirted the edge to stay in the sun and there were no jumping-trees there. So long as we lived on the farm I never wandered those woods again.

After Nelle had been shot, pitched into the woods and laid to rest, we had only Old Flory to work for us, and plowing was impossible so we depended on Walt Nester to bring his great team of "plow horses" over to till our garden. Walt charged eight dollars and usually stayed for doughnuts and lemonade after he finished work.

It bothered me to watch him sitting beside our kitchen

cupboard chomping doughnuts, slurping lemonade through his mustache and talking as though he belonged at our house. I knew we needed him and appreciated his helping us. It didn't seem right that he should act as if he owned us just because he had a good team and could make money.

Walt was a big ambling man who looked as though he had been put together from old worn-out parts, each one too big to fit any of the others. He was kind, slow of movement and gracious in his way. He wore his shabbiness and dirt as a hallmark of The Depression and as if it were a temporary condition. He always looked as though he was about to hurry home and get cleaned up, but he never seemed to get around to doing it. To look at him gave you hope and made you feel sure that some day he would emerge from his dilapidated condition all dressed up and very gallant.

All through the long Depression summer and for a long time after the garden was up and growing, Walt kept making trips to our house to collect his plowing money. I doubt he ever expected to get it. But the time must have come when he desperately needed some cash and he came over and sat himself down beside the cupboard top where Mother was washing dishes in the dishpan. He settled all his ill-fitting parts in a kitchen chair, tipped back against the wall and leaned there as if he was prepared to wait until he got his money, no matter how long it took.

After he announced, "I gotta have my money," Mother dug in her apron pocket and silently offered him the two dollars on account she had tucked there when she saw him coming across the back yard. "It's not enough," he said softly but firmly.

Mother was equally adamant, gentle but firm. "There it is. Take it or leave it."

Walt waited. Mother waited, and continued to hold out

the money in her wet, soapy hand. It seemed to me they might come to blows. I was frightened. There was something in their demeanor that I did not understand. They were arguing without either one saying a word—just looking at each other. I scuffed and kept my eyes down.

Mother dropped the bills on the floor in front of Walt and returned to her dishes. They lay there in a little, wet, crumpled pile. Walt stared at them a while then hunched himself up, gathered his ungainly physique together and ambled silently out. So far as I know, he never was paid for the plowing. It was a waiting time for him, too. That was the way it was with everyone then. People worked but few were ever paid. There was no money in circulation. No one had enough to buy much of anything.

But the whole town thought we were pretty well-off, what with two homes, a summer place on the farm and a winter place in town with Uncle Charley. It made little difference that we lived on the farm in order to feed ourselves and with Uncle Charley to keep him company during the winter. Two places made us rich.

Mrs. Morganheiser cornered me one day in their grocery store as I negotiated for some pink wintergreen candy, saying, "I guess you McNaught kids have always had whatever you wanted, haven't you?"

She seemed to be demanding not so much an answer as an explanation. Not to be outdone, I countered, "Well, there are things we would like but don't have." Which only made the situation worse.

The strained smirk on her face made me sure I had said the wrong thing so I scuffed and looked down. I was not about to give up, whatever she thought and, as usual, scuffing, looking down and waiting worked to my advantage. I got the wintergreens and scooted out of the store before she could quiz me any more about the family's finances.

I was not to be defeated. There must be some of my Mother in me—I could ignore, endure and wait.

During those lean years while Father was away trying to find work, the town seemed to think we were just dead-beats—and Mother let them. She got what she needed for us, we made it through the hard times, were happy and Father eventually got a job in a trade school in the city. We had a little money and were in a position to borrow some, not necessarily to pay bills, but to have a little cash on hand in order to live.

The Folks discussed who might be willing to finance us. (Evidently the bank was not.) We discovered a rich farmer north of town who had some money he would be willing to put out at interest. The deal went through. We got the cash and another debt.

It was immediately evident that the rich farmer was rich because he knew how to collect what was owed him. He seemed to know when Father had come home for a week-end after a payday and appeared at our front door to get each of his installments as they came due. He was not like Walt Nester. Something about his demanding attitude made it clear we had better pay, and we did.

Now, fifty years later, when I go back there and drive past that resplendent farm, it seems to be to be truly a rich farmer's place. One that got that way and stayed that way because the owner could collect when no one else dared to. I will always be able to see him standing at our door, at least twelve feet tall, very dark and very mean.

My memories of Walt Nester are soft and comforting and filled with gratitude.

ANATOMY LESSONS

Monday, October 26. It has

been a good weekend. Spent Sunday at Dave's helping him dress out some of his aged chickens. He does not remember the old hard times when there was no money to buy commercial meat and we had to learn to butcher in order to eat. So he welcomed my offer of help. Being older, my memory is longer and to me the butchering is only another necessary household chore.

Butchering time on the farm was a learning time. It was considered pretty much all right for children of our tender years, five or six, to watch chicken dressing, even to participate, while we were still so little we had to stand on The Stool in order to reach the kitchen table. Never mind that the knives were almost as long as our arms; the word simply was, "Now, don't cut yourself."

It was the large animal killing, whacking in the head with the axe, shooting, sticking and gutting that was shielded from our childish eyes. So we filled in the information on how livestock became meat by hiding in the tool-shed and squinting through the cracks in the siding where we could watch the butchering that went on in the roofed areaway between the granary and the corncrib where the hogs and cattle were killed and hauled up toward the roof to be slit from head to tail and gutted out.

When Bert and I heard Father tell Mother, "Get those kids in the house and keep them there," we knew it was about time to start and we ripped off across the backyard, through the fence, across the field by the barn and into the tool-shed where we took up our watch beside the biggest crack we could find. We knew that to Mother, "Out of sight was out of mind," and with the many chores connected with getting ready to make lard and sausage and can beef and pork, she had no time for us. She probably knew where we were anyway and left us alone to develop our minds, collect information and expand our horizons.

Father was very squeamish about butchering. He was nervous, the cattle bellowed, the pigs squealed, the neighbors yelled directions, Father's aim was usually poor, the bullets did not penetrate skulls very well and the knives for sticking were usually dull.

In the late afternoon, when he came triumphantly lugging halves of hogs or quarters of beef into the kitchen, he recounted the whole operation to Mother. It must have been therapeutic and got the unpleasantness off his mind. As he came in through the back door puffing and breathless, he said to her, "Those damn bullets are still no damn good. They just flattened out." "Damn" was about the most profane cuss word he ever used. But it served well to emphasize that it was hard enough to kill a pet farm animal for food without the bullets just dropping off the skull. It truly must have been pretty unnerving to stand there shooting repeatedly at our cow, Daisy, the old revolver banging away and dear Daisy simply standing there staring at him, dazed but not dead.

Nevertheless, Father insisted on trying to do his own killing. At least, he tried before yielding to a more experienced neighbor who knew how, grabbed the axe, hit Daisy between the eyes and made her into meat. Though inept, Father was proud. It was a mark of manhood to do your own killing—then to accept the neighbors' help with the rest of the work. Altogether, it was incredibly exciting and after Bert and I had squeezed past the hayrake and the manure spreader and settled down in the dim light beside our cracks to watch, we learned where pork and beef came from and how to prepare it as well.

Pigs were the most sensational. Their squeals while they were hauled up for sticking split the air and sent us to shivering there in the shed. I often wondered if I really wanted to watch but enduring the pig's screams for help was extremely worthwhile. I forgot Bert, forgot everything and sat there soaking up sights and sounds and information, thinking, "I could do that if I needed to," and wishing I could make a try at it.

Sometime during pig butchering, there was a brief, dull lull while Father and the neighbors scraped off the bristles. It was about like picking a chicken. They dunked the carcass into some hot water which had been heating in a big, black cauldron hung over a fire in the back yard, flopped it down on some boards laid across the sawhorses and went at the bristles with scrapers resembling flat, round potato mashers. It was not very interesting—just the very dead pig lying there, its fat and flab jiggling as the men scraped. When that job was finished, they tossed a few pails of cold well water over the carcass and it was hauled up again for cleaning.

It was a good time while the scraping was going on to dash into the kitchen for a quick snack to take back into the shed to munch on. We watched and ate and thought nothing of it except about how good fried, fresh pork and hams and bacon were going to taste. Our only thought was that now the dull scraping was done, the interesting stuff would begin again.

After the bellowing and squealing, sticking, scraping and gutting was done, the real learning started. Especially in summer when it was warm enough to sit outdoors beside a carcass to study the physiology of an animal. But it was a poor time for butchering because we had no refrigeration. I can remember Mother sitting in the hot sun on the grass in the field by the barn beside a washtub filled with a pig's total insides. And, as she sorted among the intestines separating out useful parts, she explained to me how the pig's viscera worked making pork chops and hams and bacon.

I do not remember the smell, which must have been horrendous there in the summer heat, only the fascinating story she told me and the glistening colors of what had been in the pig and was now in the tub. It seemed to me there was more in the tub than could ever have fitted inside the pig and I wondered why it needed all that in order to make hams and bacon and all the rest. Never once did Mother ever say, "This pig gave up his life so we could have meat." It was taken for granted that the pig was meant for food. That was why we worked hard to raise it. Mother's engrossing lesson surely was the principal reason I never got sick at butchering time.

That's the way life was when I was four or five or six. So now, cutting up a chicken is not distasteful. It doesn't bother me, perhaps, because I was never permitted to think it could.

CAUGHT!

Wednesday, October 28. The days
are more dark than light now. Sometimes the sun shows us a favor and shines just enough to illuminate the changing season. There is frost in the morning. Leaves are dry and rattle as they fall. Trees are almost bare. Clouds race first one way then another wherever the whim of the wind sends them. We have mud underfoot that stiffens as the sky bends down to clinch the earth in a cold embrace. It all says, "Get ready for winter." Then a bright, warm day suggests it can be put off for a while.

For us on the Old Farm, we had to get ready for winter or be cold and hungry. Food and fuel were the most important. After we had the garden in, the cabbages and potatoes stored away and the cold had come, the North Porch became our refrigerator. It held everything we needed to get us through until spring. Besides the cabbages and root vegetables in the hole under the floor, jars and crocks and all sorts of containers covered tables placed along the wall where they hugged the house and gained enough warmth to keep their contents from freezing.

An "old" solid walnut table sat there covered with crocks of pickles and pork and lard. It was known as The Walnut Table, the name recalling its former glory. Every time some adult voice importuned, "Go get a crock of pork off The Walnut Table," we were reminded of its grandeur and venerated its age. But, like everything else on the farm, utility came before splendor.

Time and humidity had warped The Walnut Table's leaves and left it disfigured and crippled, doomed to spend the rest of its days in utilitarian servitude on the cold porch. Now, many weary years later, it glorifies Adah's dining room, restored to its former shining splendor and function.

We welcomed cold weather because it meant we could "put down" some pork during butchering time. Grandmother Dorset and Father must have had some kind of a truce during butchering. Even without speaking to each other, they could work together and get a job done quickly and efficiently. A certain division of labor kept each of them occupied with a particular task and out of each other's way. Hunger can heal a lot of family feuds.

It usually was after the early winter dark, when Father and the neighbors finished butchering so the cutting-up had to be done by the pale, yellow light of an oil lamp. When the neighbors had left, carrying home shares of liver and fresh pork, Father brought in the half-a-hog (exactly half, split head through tail) and plopped it down on the kitchen table. I think he split the tail with a certain finesse so he would have exactly "half-a-hog." It must have been his little joke.

The killing and gutting never bothered me much as I viewed it through the crack in the tool-shed but the half-a-head sickened me. Its split brain seemed an emasculation of life itself. I wondered if the brain was the part where the pig really died. Nevertheless, it taught me a lot about the anatomy of a pig's skull. I was about as high as the kitchen table and could look right into each half of the head and see where the parts were as I scrouched underneath the carcass where it dangled over the edge of the table.

The pig looked pale and dead, not at all like meat. Death, not food, seemed to fill the room. There were many times when I forgot how good fresh pork tasted and wished hog cutting-up could be done in the daylight and somewhere other than on the kitchen table where we ate.

Everything was done on the kitchen table. It was continually covered with the clutter of food preparation, meat butchering, fruit preserving, baby bathing, diaper changing, sewing, letter writing and all the impedimenta of living. It was the workbench of our lives.

"Clear off the table," was the urgent cry that preceded every meal. Then came the command, "Set the table." Setting the table, eating and clearing the table were three-times-a-day chores. Always the same, it structured our days. As soon as we ate and the table was cleared, preparation for the business of living resumed. So it was at butchering time. We hardly finished our last bites of supper before Mother's frantic command splintered the evening calm, "Clear the table! Your Father's bringing in half-a-hog." And everyone scurried to get things ready for Father's cutting-up.

Our farm animals had pet names but when they became food, they lost their identity. After Daisy was finally dispatched, cut up, wrapped in part of an old sheet and hung up to cure on the North Porch, she became beef. We named the hogs and called them, "Piggy" while they were alive, but dead, they were "pork." Perhaps, it was another ruse that enabled us to devour our pets.

So, in the late evening by lamplight our "piggies" finally became food as the cutting-up began. Father was not very skilled at trimming out hams and chops and slabs of bacon but he had a Book with diagrams and directions. It was grubby and grease-stained and, as he worked away with the diagrams spread out on the half-a-hog, it became grubbier. Through the years, it had become almost illegible. Although, he depended on The Book to avoid mistakes, he often cut out queer shaped hams and chops and bacon slabs. Then he just trimmed off odd corners and added them to the pile reserved for sausage meat.

The more tired and hurried Father was, the bigger the pile to be ground up for sausage. I think he often just lopped off the more obvious cuts and let the pile of pieces grow saying, "Oh well, that will make good sausage." We always had lots of hand-ground, hand-mixed sausage that took much muscle and determination to put through our little food grinder and mix with salt and pepper and seasoning. It amounted to at least twenty or thirty pounds of Father's mistakes.

The day after he finished belonged to Grandmother Dorset who took great pride in putting down the sausage patties and chops and making the lard. She fried everything all at once—a whole hog's worth. And at the same time, she "tried out" the lard, which meant rendering all the fat from a whole pig, for it had to be taken care of and "put down" before it spoiled. She covered the top of the kitchen range with her favorite "spiders" for frying chops and side meat and all her big black iron kettles for trying out lard, while underneath, the fire roared with our best stove wood.

Grandmother had her own way of keeping an even heat, not hot enough to burn food but steady enough to get the job done in record time. Mostly, she did it by knowing when to stop turning and stirring and to put in more wood. When it was exactly the right time, she was casual and quick about it. She grabbed the side of her apron and, using it as a holder to open the hot door in the front of the firebox, shoved in a stick and never caught herself or the house on fire. The whole operation at any time until she finished would surely have caused a magnificent conflagration and terrible burns but no one seemed to think much about it. It was like "not falling down in the pigpen" and "not cutting yourself." You did not monkey around with hot grease and lard. That was Grandmother's job. You stood out of the way and watched and learned so that some day you could do it too.

After she finished, there was nothing left but the "cracklin's," good for chicken food, good for chewing. Crisp bits of delicious browned pork fat, full of flavor and calories, we gulped them down like peanuts and they never seemed to make us fat.

When the chops and sausage patties and odd pieces of pork were fried brown, Grandmother packed our crocks full of alternating layers of meat and lard. Then she carried them out to The Walnut Table on the North Porch to sit in the cold of winter. We all knew what would happen to the pork if the temperature climbed above freezing so we learned to watch the weather while still very young. Whenever we wanted pork chops, pork steak, sausage or pork pieces, someone braved the cold of the porch to bring in a crock without much of an idea of what was in it except it was sure to be more than plenty for a meal. All we had to do was dig the meat out from under the hard lard, warm it in a spider and it was ready to eat.

As the weeks went by, the pork in the crocks developed a flavor all its own, sort of a cross between rancid and spoiled, depending on the outside temperature. We ate a lot of pork during warm spells. I was at least eighteen before I found out that pork did not always have that distinctive, rancid-spoiled taste.

Making the headcheese was another of Grandmother's special chores. She usually did it late in the evening when she was too tired to stand over the stove any longer. Then she sat down near the oil lamp, held the half-a-hog's head on her lap and cut the meat off for cheese. Headcheese preparation was a bit much for me. There was something about Grandmother sitting beside the kitchen table in the faint, yellow lamplight bending over the half-a-head, cutting and slicing with her hair falling over her face and her thin, blue-veined hands going over the exposed skull to get every last bit of meat, that did not give me an appetite for headcheese or anything else. In fact, during the headcheese preparation she did not even seem to be my Grandmother. We were never without headcheese because no one ever ate it. But Grandmother never wasted anything in her whole life.

After two or three days all the pig would be put away, both halves of it. We would have learned all about butchering, cutting up and putting down and about pig anatomy, and we would eat well through the winter without meat inspection, sanitation and refrigeration, and in spite of trichinosis. Altogether, it was a tremendously interesting time, whether you are five or six, or ten or twelve, or over eighteen.

Now I think about how tired Mother and Father and

Grandmother must have been. Yet I never remember a complaint or a procrastination. They did what had to be done whenever it was needed with satisfaction and joy. They knew there was no other way.

Fuel required a year-round effort and we all helped. Like almost everything we did, it was dangerous. Trees had to be cut down and sawed into chunks, stove wood split from the chunks then hauled into the house, stacked in the woodshed and later taken down to Uncle Charley's for our winters there with him. Us Kids did it as a matter of course, just watching someone older and learning, then pitching in and doing. No one ever discouraged us by saying, "You're too little for that." Growing up was a time of watching and learning and eagerly waiting for our chance to do the job at hand.

Bert never missed an opportunity to stand around and watch and learn, his big brown eyes staring unblinkingly and his mouth open. He seemed to absorb knowledge better that way. He watched so much and learned so fast, he could do most of the heavy chores at a very early age and often did more than his share of the family's work.

It was during one of his watching and learning times while we still lived on the Old Old Farm that he was hit in the temple by a chunk of wood Father threw off the wagon on to the woodpile behind the house. As always, Mother took over with her doctoring. She had very few remedies but they were good and simple and they worked. One of her best was cold water pumped from our deep well. She filled the old tin dishpan with it and dunked in whatever was bruised or bleeding.

Mother lay Bert on the floor on the landing overlooking the woodshed, held his head above the dishpan and dipped cold water over the wound until the blood was only a trickle. Somehow she managed to bandage it with no sterile gauze, adhesive tape or prepared bandages. A piece of torn sheet, scorched on the always-hot stove to sterilize it, went next to the wound, then more torn sheet was tied around his head. It made him look gallant and brave, not unlike the newspaper pictures of World War I soldiers. A bandage in those days was extremely satisfying. When you were hurt, you really looked it and got lots of sympathy. Generally, you needed it. Mother had no aspirin among her remedies.

Bert's head healed. He has always had a gray spot there in his hair and says he can remember nothing before that time. But I have noticed through the years that he surely remembers how to do everything he found out about while standing around watching and learning with his mouth open.

Besides watching in order to learn, we experimented and practiced for the time when we could participate in all the enchanting, dangerous fun of the farm—all the more fun because it was dangerous. "Stay off the cultivator in the field by the barn," was one of the few and very firm admonitions we received.

The cultivator was high, rusty and covered with inconvenient places on which to fall. And the old, butting buck sheep lived in the field where it stood. Bert and I were fearless so the admonition was often repeated.

After supper when the summer day's fun was slipping away to leave us without much to look forward to but getting washed for bed, we frequently stood peering with longing through the high back gate at the intriguing mechanisms of the big riding cultivator and the "nice, soft, old wooly buck" who did not look as it he would hurt anyone.

Finally, our longing to try working its levers in order to "play cultivate" overcame any fear we had of being bunted, knocked down and stamped on. So one summer evening, we squeezed through the gate and made for its high seat while keeping an eye out for the old buck. I figured that with a quick scoot, I could climb up out of his reach and have a go at working the levers to raise the teeth and "cultivate" and that Bert could get aboard somewhere. He was younger and smaller and such an important job should rightfully belong to me and he would just have to ride along.

It seemed a good plan with few hitches and would be a lot of fun sitting up high out of reach of the old buck. I half hoped he would come charging along and butt the daylights out of the cultivator and imagined our hanging on for dear life and with great cunning as he tried to shake us off.

The sprint beyond the gate was uneventful and I managed to stretch my short, spindly legs enough to climb up the spokes of the wheels and mount to the seat. Bert hung on somewhere below, the old buck was a gray splotch far across the field, and our work could begin. The lack of a team of horses and planted rows was of no concern to me. We had a cultivator with things to pull and push and teeth to turn the earth. No one had noticed our absence from the back yard and we could look forward to a fine, cool evening of good work.

But the rusty levers which moved on the cogs resisted my every effort to pull them back to raise the teeth. I strained and tugged and began to worry about "ever getting this cultivating done." By now, I had the team, the planted rows, an interested and admiring passenger and nothing was stopping me from the glory of worthwhile endeavor except the sticky, stubborn levers that would not budge.

Worry about not getting the work done took hold of me. I felt the urgency of food production and the need to prove I could finish it in time to save the crop and feed the family. In my mind, I saw vicious weeds choking out the vegetables and the family starving with only my skill and bravery to save them. One look at Bert perched atop the big wheel beneath me with his dark eyes staring convinced me I had better do something pretty quick. Food for the family depended on my getting the gears in place, the teeth up and the cultivator running.

Finally, I grabbed the lifting lever with one hand, grasped the cogs with the other and, laying my thumb on the top to get a better purchase, jerked back on the lever handle. It started to move! The day was saved! Bert and the family would not starve and everyone would admire me. A final yank freed the rusty lever, raised the teeth and meshed my thumb in the corrugations of the cogs.

The team disappeared. The green, planted rows were no longer below. Bert and the family were not starving and I was caught where I was not supposed to be. The old buck would probably come and butt us off and we could not get away. There was no escape to avoid detection unless I could release the levers and free my thumb.

Some futile tugs and a lot of blood convinced me I had better let the cultivating go and scream for help. So, after thoughtfully considering the odds, I screamed. Bert shut his mouth, took a breath and yelled too. We raised the whole family. Mother and Grandmother ran from the kitchen and the supper dishes and Father came tearing down the lane, all of them surely fearing the old buck had us cornered and was busy trying to kill us.

Father got there first. I can still see him flying along, his slight, scrawny figure hitting the ground only now and then as his fear and his anger propelled him. I stopped screaming to watch him, fascinated by his airborne leaps. His legs, with feet attached, seemed to be waving underneath his body, never touching the ground except now and then to shoot him high into the air. Whenever I stopped screaming, he slowed down. So I screamed again to watch him leap again. My thumb did not hurt all that much and the attention and excitement crowded out any apprehension about the punishment that was sure to come.

The old buck was forgotten—probably having retreated to a far corner of the field to avoid the din. Father arrived with a last, gasping leap, shoved Mother and Grandmother aside and climbed up to the seat beside me. He pushed back the lever, released my thumb, picked me up, held me close and carried me toward the house and the old tin dishpan full of cold water.

It was the first time I had ever noticed my Father as a man, a conquering hero who could save me from disaster and my own foolishness. I loved and admired him for it. He made me feel protected and cherished as I snuggled against his shoulder on the way to the house and safety. Mother hurried ahead to fill the dishpan and to get the torn-sheet bandages ready. Grandmother followed behind offering advice. My bleeding was stopped and I was bandaged and got a lot of sympathy. Everybody seemed to understand I was only trying to save the family from starvation or, at least, to prove I could do it if need be.

And Father went back up the lane to finish whatever he had been doing. Not leaping and flying through the air but with slow, tired steps never knowing that for a little while, he had been my shining hero.

The farm work went on with no time for worry about infection, broken thumbs or the future. The present kept us busy with the work necessary to provide food and fuel. My injury was forgotten almost before I stopped bleeding. All that could be done for me had been accomplished. It was up to me to get well.

November

"CYCLONES"

Monday, November 2.

Fog smothers us this morning so dense the building across the street has vanished. A cardinal is snoozing in the pine outside the back bedroom window. All the world seems to be waiting for the day to get started and the day just shrugs, spits out more fog and slinks back into night.

It has been a good weekend, visiting with my brothers, their wives and children and grandchildren. We certainly are getting to be a lot of people—our Family. Now and then someone goes off to lead their own life. It is probably good. We should not cling together shivering and apprehending the future as in the past when we were so close. But it is comforting for we older ones to be together now. We have a good time reminiscing and laughing about the Good Old Days. They were good—poor but good.

We had a way of life and living that enabled us to endure: land and food and a home to shelter us. But we were awkward socially and came hurrying home whenever soci-

ety wounded us. Finally, home became the place we pre-
ferred. We thought of ourselves as Us Kids and all other
youngsters became Other Kids.

Michigan's summer storms made us cling together. They
were frightening, awesome and great entertainment.
Mother loved them and was able to enjoy their grandeur
because she was certain she knew exactly what to do when
they threatened. She had strict rules for surviving the
weather which we never disobeyed. "Never stand under a
tree when it is 'lightninging' " was her most urgent
prohibition. No matter how hard it rained, we never sought
that friendly shelter. And we stayed out of fields for she
taught us, "You will stick up in the open and be a target for
a lightning strike. Don't stand up whatever you do. Lie
down wherever you are."

We spent many of our days roaming the woods and
fields so storms usually caught us out in the open far from
shelter. She wanted to make sure we understood that lightning struck without warning, slanting from a few innocent-
looking clouds to incinerate whatever might be standing
upright: trees, farm animals and people. When it killed
Cousin Cad Farbe while he was hurrying to get his garden
plowed, she told us straight out all about it.

It happened on a gloomy, ominous day when she had
gathered us all inside to await an approaching storm that
she got the news on our crank telephone. She was sure it
was dangerous to answer the phone when it was "lightninging" but fearing trouble, she answered anyway. Us Kids
knew it must be something important for anyone to call up
during a storm and we all gathered around her waiting and
listening, certain it would turn out to be something fearful
and exciting.

We watched, tense and anxious, while Mother pressed
the receiver close to her ear, leaned her elbow on the little

shelf below the mouthpiece and said a fearful, "Hello, Mc-Naughts." Her face paled and she leaned more heavily on the little shelf, "Oh no! Oh dear me, no! It can't be!"

Then her voice got hoarse and she began to swallow a lot and we knew she was upset. She choked up, cleared her throat and we heard her say, "Oh no! When?" and "Is there any hope?"

She didn't say much more, only "Um" and "Um hum. UH UH," and, "I can't believe it!"

I was sure it must be a death. But whose? I thought of all the folks who were important to us. Of Father and Less Lawrence and all the ones we depended on to keep us content and untroubled. I began to worry about how the death of any one of them could hurt us.

Mother turned from the phone and choked out, "Cad is dead. Struck by lightning while he was plowing. They just brought him in. His whole body is burned and covered with black spots. Even his watch and suspender buckles are melted."

I was relieved in a way. We didn't depend on Cousin Cad for help with the farm work. He was only one of the town relatives who now and then stopped by for pie and cold chicken on Sunday afternoons. He spent most of his time in his lumberyard selling boards and watching over his business and was not concerned with our welfare. I sighed, quit worrying and decided that our secure farm life could go on in serene contentment.

The family discussed Cad's demise for a long while. Every time a storm came up, the conversation turned to lightning and Cousin Cad. Always the tale ended with someone making the remark, "Well, Cad never knew when to quit. He just kept on doing things to make more money no matter what." It sounded as if they felt greed had cost him his life and that he had gotten about what he deserved for being so much richer than all the rest of us.

After Cousin Cad was killed, caution and apprehension almost obliterated our reverence and awe of summer storms. But as time went on, he was forgotten and storm stories were not always concerned with grief and death. We especially loved to listen while Mother told us her most astonishing "cyclone" story about "the woman who was caught in her bathtub and lifted bare-naked, bathtub and all, into a tree," where she was forced to remain disheveled in her déshabillé until rescued. That she was bare-naked probably contributed, at that demure time, to the endurance of the yarn.

All storms, particularly tornadoes[1], were wondrous additions to our prosaic lives. After one had passed, it was a time of delightful discovery when the whole family went out to see what had been done and to listen to the neighbors' tales about trees full of clothes, buildings lifted and set down far from their foundations, cattle, sheep, hogs and horses tossed about like chips and feathers, whole fields of wheat and oats and hay "down." Laid so flat by the wind and rain that the crop was lost, for it never could be cut with a reaper. Once in a while, we found an animal lying dead in a pasture or under a tree where it had taken shelter. And, we were reminded again of Mother's prohibitions and of Cousin Cad.

"Lie down in a ditch," was her rule for "cyclones." It was quite simple, "If it is 'lightninging,' get out of the open and don't stand under a tree." And, "If the wind blows, lie down in a ditch." Mother generally added, "Flat!" for emphasis as she explained, " 'Cyclones' will usually jump over a depression and you will be safe lying flat in a ditch." We never questioned Mother's 'lightninging' and 'cyclones.' We knew

[1]We always called them cyclones.

what she meant and that was enough.

She continually cautioned us, "Watch the southwest; run to the nearest ditch; don't wait for your coat. *Take the Twins!* No matter where you are, *lie down flat in a ditch!*"

Everywhere we went, I kept an eye out for a ditch in case it was needed and often dreamed of how exciting it would be lying there with the wind howling over me and the rain coming down while I outwitted the storm. It seemed as if it would be nice and cozy but very wet.

"Getting wet" had a special stigma in those days. Perhaps because we had no way of drying things except outdoors on the clothesline. When your clothes got wet for any reason, you frequently had to "wear them to dry out." I decided to avoid getting wet at whatever the cost.

Getting ready when it began to cloud up before a summer storm was almost more exciting than the storm itself. Early summer was "cyclone" season and each time a hot, still, sultry day came, Mother assembled us on the North Porch to watch and wait. While the clouds were gathering, her cautions and admonitions brought us to an unbelievable state of excitement and terror—a wonderful mixture of joy and fear.

"Now, don't go away. Stay in the house. Where are the Twins? Get the Twins!" she kept repeating. Pewee and Bert each rounded up a Twin. It was standard procedure before any important family event to "get the Twins" who were usually found in one of their favorite hiding places pursuing their own diversions.

Mother never failed to pile our coats in a handy spot where we could grab them and run, and to put out a good supply of food in case the wait should be a long one. She knew a chewing child is a contented one and that, as long as the food held out, she would have no problem keeping all five of us under her protection.

"It's coming up fast!" was always followed by, "Get your coats on! Sit down!" It was better than a circus. Everybody eating as many last bites as they could hold, scrambling and shoving to get a good seat, crumbs flying, a few squabbles starting and Mother, as always, "rising to the occasion."

Although we were terrified, at the same time, we felt secure for we knew exactly what to do. So long as we lay "flat in a ditch" and did not "stand in the open or under a tree" we would be safe. It made us feel capable and indomitable and in control of the storm's threat to our security.

From our house on the hill, we could see the black clouds building in the west. A quick, cool breeze came then died. It was so quiet we could hear the dead leaves rattle on the old apple trees in the North Field.

Before "she hit," the animals became restless. All but the chickens who kept on picking up bits of gravel, grain and bugs while the wind riffled their feathers the wrong way making them look like Grandmother's feather dusters.

The six big pines in the front yard began to moan, getting ready to roar. It was one of our particular joys to stand safely on the front porch listening to their grand storm song and watching their branches bend to the ground in defiance of the wind. Knowing pines would bend and not break was another fact that made us feel knowledgeable and superior.

When the wind quit in the quiet before the storm and the black clouds seemed to stop in the sky, we all waited, sure something fearful and destructive was about to happen. Mother checked us over to make sure we were well buttoned up and commanded again, "Get the Twins," and went over the familiar routine, "Now, if it strikes, run to the nearest ditch and lie down flat." It would have been prudent to run to the ditch before it struck, but we would have "gotten wet" for nothing. So we waited, kept warm and dry and got ready to sprint to the ditch when, and if, Mother should command, "Go!" In the meantime, we enjoyed the storm, munched the food and scuffled.

Mother left it to us to pick the ditch. It was a tribute to our judgement and a credit to her teaching. It made us feel independent and proud, confident that we could follow the rules and use them to our best advantage. She accepted our childish squabbling and scuffling but she expected us to think like wise, rational human beings.

While we waited there on the North Porch, we kept our eyes glued to the old apple trees dotting the North Field so as not to miss the sight of one blowing down. We knew their every branch and twig and all the weak spots in their trunks and realized that, sooner or later, they were bound to go. They were old friends and we dreaded their eventual loss. We had spent long hours perched among the leaves in their tops contemplating life, watching bugs and birds and exchanging secrets. When the world seemed rotten and we wanted to get away from someone or something, or hide out to escape an anticipated confrontation, we scurried into the North Field and climbed an apple tree.

One by one the storms had claimed our best climbing-trees until only four were left. We loved the excitement of one overturning but hated to think of it going. For all our years, they had stood by us holding out their branches in welcome to comfort and rejoice with us. They offered us a place to go which is what everyone needs. It was thrilling to watch them fall before the storm but sad to see them lying dead with their roots sticking up in the air.

Usually the storms arrived with a great wind going over our hill which sent chips and chicken feathers, straw and old papers flying past the North Porch. (A really good farm then always had lots of interesting junk around.) We watched and hoped the apple trees would stand firm and listened while the pines in the front yard roared their mighty challenge. Just before the rain came, there was a flash of lightning immediately followed by a crash of thunder. Then we all chorused, "That was close," for we had been taught to count the seconds between the flash of light and the crash of thunder. Every second was a mile away and when they came at the same time, "That was close."

When the rain started blowing in sheets across the North Field, the air turned cold and the storm "settled in." We sat quietly then, shivered and sighed, a little disappointed that it would soon be over and all the grand display of God's might come to an end for another time.

After the rain stopped and only the "spanking" of drops from trees and rooftops opened chinks in the after-storm stillness, the animals came out and went back to their barnyard business. Chickens pecked about for tidbits, walking carefully, planting their newly-washed yellow feet in the mud, holding their tails drooped down and bobbing their heads as if to shake the water off their soggy feathers. Cattle and pigs, more curious than hungry, left the comfort of the barn and the shed to step gingerly about in the mud and manure, their hooves making sucking, smacking noises as they pulled them out of the soft ooze. The sheep nibbled at the tender grass, found it to their liking and wandered off down the lane.

All the farm smells, intensified by the wet, became more noticeable, smelling not necessarily clean but different than they had before in the dry heat. Everything smelled like what it really was: the chickens' wet feathers, like the dirt and dust where they had waddled to kill their lice, the hogs and cattle and sheep gave off their strong animal smells, all the goodness of growing vegetables came from the garden. And manure smelled like ammonia and rotting things. A barnyard after a rainstorm with steam rising from every refuse pile and each indentation filled with yellowish, brown liquid (fine for fertilizer and unbelievably foul) is really a barnyard.

When the sun came out, we took up our day wherever we had left it and redirected our fun to employ the residue of wind and water. Generally it meant building dams in the now-flooded ditch along the road by the front yard. And getting wet.

Perhaps we were a little disappointed nothing catastrophic had happened and that the storm hadn't turned out to be a "cyclone," but we had been shaken to our shoetops and once more impressed with the importance of watching the southwest for copper-colored clouds, never standing in the open or under a tree, of being ready to run when the wind came and of lying flat in a ditch.

Never in my life have I taken refuge under a tree during a storm. Never either, have I had to lie flat in a ditch. But long ago I was taught to do it and still could if need be.

Weather was a fascinating part of our lives. It told us when we could do what we wanted to do. It was a force greater than anything else and held us in its power. We loved it and watched its beauty and its frightening might. We complained about it and discussed it. It grew our food and threatened to take it away. It furnished snow and ice, and rain and wind, and soft dark nights, all for our own special delights.

Weather was a formidable foe and we enjoyed our battles with it knowing we never could be the winner but that, with courage and dexterity, we could overcome the worst threats it had to offer. It was our friend: we depended on it to change the seasons, to offer warmth and cold, moist and drying winds for growing times, and resting times for the soil.

We were never alone out there in the country. We could always watch the weather. And we had each other.

SHOOTING THE OLD FORD

Monday, November 9.

Today is one of those nice sunny ones that have no business coming along at this time of year. They glisten and tease and remind us of what we soon will be missing. Days like this make me suspicious about what is coming. They are too nice to last. They give no indication of what their intentions are. They give me false hope. They are like some people I know who are too pleasant. I don't quite trust them.

Today demands that I make the most of it and makes me feel guilty if I do not. I usually look back on nice days and wonder what I ever did with them and curse myself for not having done more.

Days like this are dull and uninteresting and make me glad to see clouds come up. Clouds have meaning, portend something definite and invite speculation. Soft, dark days with clouds lure me into tranquil loafing and make me want to enjoy the weather, not feel I have to use them up. One knows what to do about clouds, not so with a too-nice day. It is Fall now and this brightness of earth and sky should not come along grinning.

Nice sunny days on the farm were days to escape from the house, the barns, the yard and work. After doing the morning and night chores, it was best to flee because, if you hung around, somebody was sure to give you a job. All adults seemed to feel that a nice day should be consumed in some worthwhile activity.

Bright, cloudless days were invariably used for cleaning the yard, the stables or the chicken coops. Somehow, a stable or a chicken coop loses all of its charm as it sits and reeks under a hot roof, sweltering in the sun.

The best thing to do on a nice sunny day is escape to

your favorite branch on your favorite tree and sit there in the cool shade with all the troubles of the world below you and only God's serene heaven above. If your tree bears fruit, you can eat green, or almost ripe, apples, try to find ripe cherries, pick pitch from the trunk to chew and sit there contentedly munching and thinking happy thoughts.

In the Old Farm days, we each had our own branch on one of the back yard trees, not chosen by lot, just agreed upon. Mine was a big, curved one on a small cherry tree, easy to climb, easy to sit on, close to the house and well-hidden by leaves. Being close to the house was an advantage. If someone called, "Henny, what are you doing? Come in and help," I could scramble down in a hurry acting like an eager, willing worker or stay out of sight, safe from becoming conscripted labor. By peeking through the leaves, I could judge what was going on and make a prudent decision as to the most advantageous course to pursue.

My comfortable perch may have been a concession on the part of my brothers who knew I dared not climb high, never having made it above the first rung of the ladder leading to the great wheel on the top of the windmill. Bertie could, and did, climb there to oil the wind motor which was activated when the big blades turned. It was another time when Us Kids did whatever had to be done.

Bert was a real climber. Somewhere he had heard about a "human fly" and practiced trying to become one, even climbing up the outside of the house from the ground to above the upstairs windows. He usually rehearsed in secret then demonstrated while Mother watched, torn between admiration and wanting to scream. It is a credit to her that she admired our escapades, even encouraged us to develop dexterity and fearlessness and only murmured soft caution while she watched, trusting us to remain unscathed. She must have given a lot of thought to how much Dr. Nevell charged for setting broken bones and sewing lacerations.

We had many things for fun and games but sports equipment presented a financial problem for which we had no solution. The front of the house with its protruding window sills was fairly asking for human fly feats. We had swings and knotted ropes hung from the barn beams or the front yard trees for trapeze stunts. Bert and I used family shotguns and rifles as a matter of course in order to kill game to eat. But they were tools for living, not for sports and shells were too expensive to be wasted on target practice. We never wandered far from home, hiking and hunting for food, without carrying a .22 rifle, a supply of fishhooks, a length of string, a few angleworms for bait in our pockets, and a hunting knife stuck in the straps of our boots. If we came across something edible: squirrels, rabbits, fish or plants, we shot it, stuck it, caught and cleaned it or dug it up. It was joyous fun tramping the woods and fields hunting for food or shooting varmints like weasels and crows but it was not a recognized sport.

About everything Bert and I saw or read about we imitated and when he made us each a bow with arrows, Mother almost lost her patience. Somewhere among the many family books, Bert read about a "stout hickory bow" such as used by English knights and Hiawatha. To him it must have seemed the ultimate weapon: cheap, efficient and to be had for the making. Hickory trees grew in the back pasture, there were a few tools in the barn, he had a lot of imagination and some information. So Bert began his great hickory bow and arrow project.

The bows he envisioned, one for each of us, would be large and lethal. There was no sense in making one that was not as effective as a .22. Arrows could be made as deadly as shells, were cheaper and could be used more than once.

During the summer, he cut the hickory, dried and seasoned it in the attic along with the drying walnuts and pop-corn, carved the bows and arrows and we made plans to shoot. Whenever I could escape from Mother and Grand-mother and housework, Bert and I were natural partners. We considered the Twins and Pewee "too little" and con-cerned only with little kid things, not with providing food for the family.

The bows turned out well. They were about five feet long and had great power. It took a mighty tug to "pull" one, but the results were spectacular. Bert made the arrows to withstand the power of the bows. He carved them from some "old pine boards" he found in the barn and tipped them with spent brass rifle shells about three inches long, retrieved from some long-ago, shooting war to which the family had sent their best men.

Stringing the bows required exceptionally strong cords or "sinews." So having none, we invented them. Uncle Charley offered us some linen twine he was not using which we could braid and wax with beeswax and make ac-ceptable sinews. Soon we had stout hickory bows, well strung, with long, strong arrows and were ready to hunt.

We had just one problem. Rabbit and squirrel hunting with bows was more stalking and walking than shooting. A rifle was more effective and a shotgun couldn't miss. We did not want to take a chance with the bows and maybe have to give up boasting about what great shots we were. Bert could shoot the eye out of game and never spoil the meat, but we had to practice with the bows and shooting at nothing was unproductive. Besides, we had to chase after the arrows which usually got lost in the grass and weeds. We did not particularly want to make a target. That seemed unproduc-tive too.

It was not long before the day came when there was no work to do and we were able to solve the problem. We went out in the North Field where the grass was not too long so we would not lose our precious arrows, and shot at each other. We were very careful, each one taking a turn shooting while the other one watched where the arrows went, gathered them up and shot them back. We were sure if we stood far enough apart there would not be much danger in getting hit. Anyway, we could see an arrow coming and duck.

Our solution lasted only long enough for Mother to spy us from the North Porch and shout, "That's enough! Stop that now. Go find something else to shoot at." We did, and started shooting at the barn door. In order to tell how good our aim was at knotholes and stains, we stood close enough for the brass-tipped arrows to cut a neat, deep dent in the door. We didn't have to chase them, they sort of bounded back to us.

Days went by. Nobody shouted, "Stop that!" We got pretty good and longed for an audience in order to demonstrate our skill and the great strength of the bows Bert had made.

Came a nice sunny day with the sun smiling down through the front yard pines on to the lawn and dappling the Old Ford which had been pulled into the shade under the catalpa tree. The yard looked cool and inviting and seemed a grand place to hold our demonstration.

"Come out, Ma," we cried. "Come out and see!"

She came out the front door, wiping her hands on her apron and wearing her questioning, worried look, probably expecting another human-fly exhibit or a new trapeze trick in the swing.

Bert and I stood at the ready, arrows in place, bows drawn and muscles straining. But there was nothing to shoot at except the pines and the catalpa tree which did not seem very satisfying.

I swung my bow around, looked for a suitably impressive target, drew a sight on the Old Ford, imagined the great "ping" a hit would make on its fender, felt sure it wouldn't do much damage and shouted, "Look Ma, how strong these bows are!" And shot the back window out of the Old Ford. There was a crash, the tinkle of falling, shattered glass and awful silence.

Mother just stood there. She did not say a thing. Just wiped her hands on her apron and walked back into the house.

Bert and I realized it was about the end of the stout hickory bow and arrow project and crept dismally back to the barn to think it over and discuss how much our garage man, Dick Dunck, would charge to fix the Old Ford's window.

Somehow, it was done quite soon. Probably to save the Old Ford's upholstery from the ablutions of summer storms. We suffered no punishment. Mother must have felt it was just another of the gambles she took when she encouraged her creative children to innovate. And we went back to shooting the barn door.

Mother never failed to watch our demonstrations with obvious pride and encouragement. She did not worry about guns and knives for she was sure we respected them and knew their use. It was seldom that she ever prohibited us from any of our innovations. I guess she just let us go and hoped for the best, knowing full well we would learn by doing and that learning was the most important thing of all.

Maybe too, she was very tired. It was impossible to watch over all five of us all the time. On bright sunny days, she must have hoped for some quiet rainy ones when we would swing from the beams in the barn, jump in the haymow or read in the attic. I doubt Mother cared very much for nice sunny days either.

PANTHERS ON THE ROOF

Wednesday, November 18.   The hazy, quiet fall days slip tranquilly by—very good for loafing, procrastinating and catching up on odd jobs. They are filled with friends and relatives who stop by to chat and we laugh about the old difficult days when life was a struggle. Time has taken those long-ago hardships and hurts and made them into tales to be savored and glorified, repeated with joy and nostalgia and, finally, at last, doubted. We have a fine collection of them. Like many Michigan families, we have a Panther Story we repeat as the truth, believe in our hearts and doubt with our intellect.

Evenings on the Old Old Farm when the wind moaned through the branches of the ancient trees beside the house and the deep dark came to surround us, were sure to bring about a retelling. Sometimes it was about a "catamount," sometimes, a "painter." But we all knew exactly what it was—a fierce, large carnivore that stalked livestock, and on occasion, people, and killed for the sport of killing.

Great Grandmother Dorset is said to have dispatched a panther with her stove poker as it prowled on the roof of the log cabin she and Great Grandfather had built under a big maple tree across our road. Their cabin was long gone but the tree still stood there and made the story vividly real to me.

In Mother's version, Great Grandfather hitched the team to the wagon and went to Fillson, the nearest town some thirty miles away to bring back a millstone and supplies leaving Great Grandmother and the children alone in the cabin. The thirty-mile trip took a week or more what with few, if any, roads, stops along the way to exchange news and gossip and a bit of a celebration while in town. Great

Grandmother was left alone to gather her own wood, keep the fire going, take care of the livestock and the family and get along alone until her man returned.

She did quite well in the daytime but at night, the panther jumped on the roof where she could hear him padding around. It must have angered her more than it scared her for, as Mother said matter-of-factly, "She took the poker and went out and killed it."

The panther tale gave me a lot of respect for Great Grandmother and an ardent desire to be as brave and capable as she, even though the shivers went up my back every time I looked across the road at the place where the cabin had stood beneath the maple tree. As each of our country evenings turned into pitch black night, I kept an eye out for panthers that might be lurking about the yard ready to pounce on our roof. Night noises turned into padding footsteps overhead and, by straining my ears, I could hear claws scratching above me. Admiration for Great Grandmother's bravery saved me from complete hysterical collapse. I felt, if she could be so courageous, I could be nothing less.

Sharing stories by the fire was a family evening rite when we gathered together in the small circle illuminated by our one kerosene lamp with the shadows hovering behind us all around the fringes of the living room. The yarns gave us great joys and frights and delightful thrills and established family traditions of daring and bravery.

Mother's experiences as a child growing up in the Michigan countryside before the turn of the century, were as good or better than those she repeated about Great Grandmother. They usually began: "When I was a little girl and everybody was sitting beside the fire at night..." which identified us quickly with the story for we would be sitting around the fire in the same house in the same living room where she had been sitting so long ago. Mother set up an impressive background for her stories about life in that house on the Old Old Farm. It seemed as if nothing of much consequence ever happened there unless "everyone was gathered around the lamp at night with the wind blowing and the rain (or snow or sleet) pelting on the windows."

Through the years, the stories grew with us and kept us entranced. Again, "It was a rainy, stormy night when Bert was little and I was rocking him in the North Room in that rocker when I heard it." And Mother pointed to the old family rocker still sitting in the North Room.

"It was like a scream. And something was hitting the house."

While Mother began the old familiar setting, the shivers started to rip up and down my spine and a cold spot came between my shoulder blades. I could hear the rain against the window, the wind and the scream and hear "it" hit the house.

Mother waited for the setting of her yarn to become truly effective, then she shifted about in her chair to hold her evening mending closer to the lamp, squinted a little to see better and went on, "I couldn't hear it very well with the wind and rain but it kept coming every time when the wind died down." She kept on building the details into a really good shiver. Each telling made the story better, more fearful and wonderful.

At last, she concluded, "It must have been a pair of loons lost in the storm being blown against the gable of the house."

For fifty years I felt apprehensive about loons and panthers. And not until I visited a lovely Northern Michigan lake and looked and listened to the flute-like call of a loon to his mate, as they paddled toward me in a truly friendly fashion, did I ever stop shivering about loons.

Never having met a panther face to face, I still quake

over them and half expect one to be somewhere out in the bushes around the house. Maybe one day we will meet, some old panther with but few teeth and me, and get acquainted.

Spring on the farm brought out some lovely local tales about, "Up the North Road." It was truly a time of renewal, for shedding a few layers of winter clothing, surreptitiously leaving off long-legged underwear, and sitting around to wait for the snow to melt and the mud to dry up.

"Up the North Road" as "In the Northwoods" was a very special place. Like the names of many places in those days of no street address, its description was its name, telling us what and where it was. The North Road was the mile North of the South Road. It needed no other designation. We lived between the two of them and that was enough. It was a witching place where all sorts of fearful and mysterious happenings occurred. Some of Mother's most interesting and astonishing tales were located there. It was where the Old Lady lived who fed her children chopped hair and molasses for a spring tonic.

I pictured the Old Lady, surrounded by her children sort of like the Old Woman in the Shoe, cutting bunches of hair off their heads and "chopping" it up with a pair of shears. Sometimes I could see her trying to chop the hair with a knife, probably on her breadboard. After some experimentation with one of our kitchen knives and my own locks, I discarded the idea as impracticable and decided shears would be better.

The Doals lived in the last house up the North Road. Beyond them was the "end of the road," a place few people ever visited and from which countless and enthralling yarns came out. Probably no one ever went there because the road was impassable and disappeared into an old, dying, neglected woodlot. Once a good yarn came out, no one ever went to check and it kept getting better with every repetition.

Nabby and Clare Doal were like skinny Jack Spratt and his fat wife. She was fat and he was thin. She was so fat it was said that when the doctor had tried to operate on her to take out her gallbladder, he had to cut through three inches of fat to get at her malfunctioning innards. As long as he was in there, he decided to remove some of Nabby's fat. Of course, as soon as she got home and recovered, she ate her way back into her old familiar chubby self.

It furnished the neighborhood with wonderful conversation and speculation as to how soon Nabby would regain her original shape and then, "What would happen if she ever had to have another operation?" The doctor would have to cut through layers of fat again and, if Nabby ever ate her way back yet another time . . . It went on and on for years with folks speculating about Nabby eating and the doctor cutting off fat in a never-ending and losing struggle. It didn't matter to me about their physiques, they were kind and tried to cheer our lives with small gifts. Nabby could tat and I spent many happy afternoons watching her as she sat overflowing her favorite rocking chair tatting out beautiful lace rings all hitched together with little circles and loops.

Once on my birthday, she fixed me three soda crackers decorated with four brown apple seeds sewn into each of their centers. I really didn't know what they were supposed to be but I loved them and looked at them often and never ate them. Perhaps she had some thought of mice and mouse bits on the crackers because mice were forever getting into our cracker jar. Grandmother Dorset must have thought so too for when I unwrapped them, she sniffed and said, "Nabby most probably was making mouse bits." Nevertheless, they were beautiful to me. I never dared to ask what they were supposed to be. Just put them away with my other treasures: some pieces of old ribbon, a doll that needed new eyes, a few brightly colored stones, and often looked at them while I thought of fat Nabby tatting and rocking and making something for me.

Mother used the North Road to inform me further about the intimacies and requirements for sex and procreation. One day while we sat in the sun by the south window having a purely scientific conversation about a virgin birth, she observed that such a thing was possible and assured me, "There was a woman up the North Road who gave birth to a baby without ever having been near a man."

It did not seem so astonishing to me that the woman had the baby all by herself but the idea of "near" was undefined and gave me cause for much conjecture. I had absolutely no idea what Mother meant by "near." Near was near such as: "passing by near a man," or a "man passing by near to me" and envisioned a sort of pollination taking place. I could see a skinny man walking along the dusty wagon track of the North Road and passing near a fat woman (probably Nabby and Clare in my mind) with his pollen flying about in a sort of yellow cloud and specks of it falling on her when she was ripe for pollination. Farm life had taught me that readiness is vital to fertilization. So much for Mother's fine example of procreation.

Then there was an Old Lady Up the North Road who could move dishes on her cupboard shelves while sitting in her rocker across the room. This revelation followed a serious discussion about Tibetan monks' ability to levitate. I have though of Tibet as being more or less like up the North Road ever since.

I imagined the nice Old Lady sitting rocking and moving her cups and saucers up and down on her shelves while she sat and rocked and smiled a smile that looked more like a grin or a smirk. I was very fond of the Old Lady and often thought about her sitting in her rocker dressed in a dark, full-skirted dress with a white lace collar, her tiny, black laced shoes just sticking out from under her skirt as she pushed herself back and forth rocking and smirking and hopping her cups and saucers up and down. I thought she probably had to do it most of the day every day in order to keep in practice and perhaps work up to something larger like pots and pans. A talent such as hers certainly would be worth cultivating.

I could see the cups, each sitting on its saucer, in a row on the shelf and considered her need to cause them to hop straight up and straight down with the saucers following the cups and the cups following the saucers down, lest they get mixed up and fall crashing to the floor, which certainly would be a great deterrent to her prowess.

I took Mother's wonderful yarns about happenings up the North Road as gospel truth. I did not think she made them up and she never said anyone had told them to her. She seemed to believe them with all her heart and delighted in passing on the information.

Mother never really thought that some things just could not be. Anything was possible. At least, anything was possible "up the North Road." It was as if many things rattled around in her head colliding with her everyday thoughts about running a house, home and kids until some absolutely fascinating, slumbering story got knocked out. She simply had to get rid of it in order to make room for more. Her yarns were like voiced, rambling thoughts. She needed to spin them out in order to go on with her day's work. They helped her escape the monotony of housekeeping and to dream away at life.

I love the Old Yarns that have made me a part of the family's past. They are the cement that glues our generations together.

NO HUGGING TIME LEFT

Friday, November 27. Morning came along today, took a look around and went grumbling back to bed. There is supposed to be a big winter storm brewing out in the West. It will be a relief when it gets here, then we can settle down to shoveling snow.

Snow-shoveling gives me a wonderful sense of accomplishment. Maybe it is because I can see what I have done, the piles offering evidence of my achievement. So far this weekend we have not been walloped with our usual Thanksgiving storm, just rain, drizzle and dark making it nice to stay in beside the fire.

Bert and Adah invited me for the day. They are kind and keep me involved as an active member of the family. Adah made her usual fabulous dinner. "Only simple turkey and trimmings," she said. But she is too modest. A meal like that for twelve people cannot be done without much careful planning and hard work. Adah is well organized and so experienced she gets a big holiday dinner almost casually, always going by the book and never having a failure.

Adah's cooking is like her personality: precise and exactly according to the rules. It gives her security and assures her success. The uncertain results of creativity have never been for Adah. If a mistake is made in a meal, it is the fault of the food or the equipment. She does her best and never even considers failure. She is a happy, bustling cook and it is a joy to eat there.

Our Thanksgivings have changed through the years. The family gathers now in smaller groups. Each one of Albert's and Lorinda's offspring meet with their own families for their separate Holidays. Us Kids are scattering, each to his own hearth and children, and we have become the Old

Folks. I wonder if the ones coming along today will be as close as we have been. I know for certain they will not have as much fun.

We have all mellowed and are more charitable and less competitive now and enjoy just being together. It is a little dull though. Those other times of competing against each other and all adults were exciting and gloriously satisfying. After family dinners, we ran in every direction that our wild ways took us, hiking, hunting, skiing and "tearing around." Now we eat and wonder what to do the rest of the afternoon. So we play sedentary games and snooze. It is impossible to work up an appetite for leftovers sitting around playing backgammon.

Still there is more to the day than food and boredom. We are each thankful in our own personal and private way. We do not talk about it. Conversation can resurrect old wounds and bring grief as well as gratitude.

We think about the ones who are gone and of the ones who are about to go and do not mention that this may be the last Thanksgiving for some of us. We only consider it a blessing we can live the day through without remembered or anticipated sadness. Our Thanksgivings could easily become days of dwelling on the past and killing hope of the future.

We visit with Laurane and Phillip and their children. No one mentions her cancer. She is getting fatter as she eats through her days enjoying the comfort that food brings. No one says to her, "My you look good. You are really gaining weight." We know weight will not help. Instead of asking her how she feels, we hug her as though to hold her for a little longer. We all know there isn't much hugging time left.

So we find comfort along with Laurane in touching and eating, knowing we are helpless to change what is to be. We each have to face our separate tomorrows no matter what they may portend. Other lives will go on even while life is ending for some of us. Thanksgiving becomes the panacea that enables us to accept our sorrow and our joy.

December

NOT SO BAD BEING BLIND

Tuesday, December 1. My days drift by, each one more alone than the ones before. But I do not mind and am able to look forward to the quietness. Right now, I piece the alone-days and the people-days together to form a good life. I look back to yesterday. It started quietly: some housework, some writing and a lot of looking at the dusty furniture sitting grim and dull in the early morning sun.

Amy called early for more help with her English papers which had to be corrected and turned in before the end of the term. I did not particularly want to pick her up to bring her here for lunch and work, but then, reminded myself she is blind and cannot see the teacher's comments. She can only sit and wait until someone reads them to her. Helping her seemed the most important thing of all.

One of the wonderful things about Amy is that she permits me to be selfish. I forget to pity her. She makes me treat her as a regular kid. She never calls and asks for help. Her breezy, friendly voice is both a salutation and an amenity, "Aunt Hen! How are you?"

We visit a while then she says, "I'm still working on my English teacher. She has given me more corrections." She does not say, "I got my English themes back with more corrections and cannot tell what they are because I can't see them." About now, my self-centered, old-lady nature topples before my conscience and my love. I entertain some wicked thoughts about English teachers and rush off to the campus to pick her up where I find her sitting in the lobby of the dorm with a big box holding a Christmas wreath she has selected for me. More evidence she is thoughtful, kind and generous.

After we finish one paper, she sorts through her notebook and gets out another theme. I am astounded. The afternoon is almost gone. We have been working hours so we finish this one in a hurry. She riffles through her notebook again where she has everything placed for easy finding and comes up with yet another one titled: "It's Not So Bad Being Blind." It recounts her ability to overcome her lack of sight and writes about the funny things that have happened and of how she wants to be known as Amy McNaught not as "that blind kid."

Twilight settles in. We have tea and chat. She shares her store of campus jokes with me and we laugh together. Dave and Em come by and we have more tea and cookies. Amy eats no cookies. She keeps her beautiful figure. When Dave and Em leave, Amy goes to the door with them to say a gracious, "Good Bye." It's another one of the things she does to put people at ease about her blindness.

At last we pack up her things and head back to the campus and the dorm. In the gathering winter dark, I get home and settle down with the evening news and try to avoid an early snooze so I can be awake when my neighbor is to call for her daily papers which I have been collecting in her absence.

No use. I leap joyfully into my flannel nightgown and old robe and am "out" on the couch before the evening TV news is over. When her knock wakes me, I stagger guiltily to the door give her the papers and make lame excuses for being asleep at seven o'clock. I decide truth is the best defense and say, "It is so cold I got into my flannel nightgown and snuggled down on the couch."

She is sympathetic, "Yes, it sure is getting colder." I invite her to come in and visit, hoping she will go away. It is good to hear her say, "Thanks, but I have to do my wash. I've been away so long everything is dirty."

"Yes, that is the way when you go away." I go on with the inane conversation thinking it must sound pretty stupid and am almost back to sleep on my feet.

She disappears down the hall toward the laundry. I lock and bar the door, slide a small table against it for extra protection and make a beeline back to the couch. I haul the old black afghan up to my chin and think, "It's been a good day although nothing very unusual happened. Maybe I should stay awake a while longer and enjoy it.

It does not matter. I am content. Sleep on the couch is the best way to spend a cold evening. I shall go right on getting into my nightgown and old friendly robe while it is still daylight and try to make acceptable excuses to anyone who is still up at six or seven and may stop in.

Probably the best excuse of all would be to say, "I'm old and tired and like to sleep."

January

SPIT

Wednesday, January 6. The New Year was a quiet one for me. I did not fight to keep awake to see the old year out. No dressing up or wondering what to wear and where to go, no struggle to celebrate, just napped while the evening drifted into night.

All Holidays were times for dressing up on the Old Farm. "Getting Ready" was a ritual we conscientiously practiced before we went anywhere. Carefully observed, it assured us we would be clean and properly attired. When Mother called us, "Come and get ready. Stop that and get ready. Now!" we knew our romping was at an end and the ceremony was about to begin. We knew too, washing would be at a minimum and getting ready completed only by the strategic application of spit.

In a house with no running water, spit was our ever ready and always available solvent, disinfectant, dampener, cleaner and hair curler. Whenever a little moisture was needed for any purpose, we used spit. If water in quantity

---

was required, it had to be dipped out of the water pail or pumped from the cistern into the washpan and carried to wherever it was to be used. Cistern water was precious to us because it was soft and would make a suds. Very little soap could be dissolved in our hard well water. Even Grandmother's homemade soft soap did nothing but float around in a scum.

Although cistern water was readily available from the kitchen pump, we used it sparingly and never drank it. It was for dish and hair washing and, in small quantities, for people washing, never bathing for we could not be sure when we would run out. The only uncontaminated water in the house was what we carried in from the well in the water pail. It was the same sort of regulation ten-quart galvanized pail we used for everything else and stood with its dipper on a shelf at the end of our dry sink opposite the pump that brought rain water up from the cistern which was buried in the ground outside the kitchen window. The water smelled like rotting vegetation and the wooden shingles on the roof where it was collected to run down through the eaves-trough into the cool depths below.

The cistern was deep and dangerous. Hand dug and walled with tile, it held our only supply of soft water. During dry times in summer, the cry went out, "Don't use cistern water until it rains." And in winter, we waited anxiously for a thaw.

The caution excited Us Kids' sense of duty to the family's welfare and gave us a good worthwhile reason to test the depth of the water to see how much we had available. Often, more out of curiosity than need, we took the wooden cover off, leaned over the edge and squinted down into the slimy, buggy blackness to judge the water level.

"Hollering down the cistern" gave us a better idea of the amount it held. If our "holler" sounded hollow and echoed back to us, we knew it was about empty. The less echo, the fuller we judged it to be. It was another game, born of necessity and a serious activity we carried on to serve our needs.

We hollered down the cistern for fun and on a dare. Somehow Mother knew when we were doing it only for fun, rapped her wedding ring on the kitchen window to gain our attention and called, "Put the cover back and stay away from it!" She appreciated our concern for the family's water supply but knew from local tragedies that recovering a drowning child from a cistern was difficult and usually futile.

After we put the cover back, we tried to get the same diagnostic results by stomping on the boards of the cover and listening to the reverberations. The noise always brought another one of Mother's raps on the window and her command, "Stay *off* the cover!" And, as a last resort she added, "Go and play," which opened many possibilities and meant we were not about to be called to do chores.

We tested the water level frequently and thoroughly and felt it to be a really worthwhile task and much more fun than feeding the animals or hoeing thistles out of the cornfield. It was our meager supply of water that gave rise to our dependence on spit.

The night before any important occasion, Grandmother Dorset captured me to "put up" my hair. It was a vital part of her struggle to make me fit to be seen in the company of our more sophisticated and well-curled town cousins and she was certain curled hair was a sure way to do it. At least, it gave her something to do so she would not be forced to sit by and watch me go off into the social fray with my hair straight and flying and my socks falling down. She must have felt attention to my top would keep folks from noticing the rest of me.

In the late afternoon, when I saw Grandmother gather her supply of hair-rags and settle down in a low chair by the parlor window, I knew it was time to "begin to get ready" and that I would have to submit. She sat spraddle-legged, stood me between her knees, caught me by the shoulders to position me just right and began the putting-up, always with the firm admonition, "Now stand still." If I wiggled, she squeezed her knees together, held me immovable and never slowed her work with the rags.

Moisture was necessary in order to achieve a respectable curl so Grandmother used spit. Her work had a sort of rhythm. She grabbed a lock of my stringy, stubborn hair, pulled it tight, spit on it, rubbed the spit around a little, then rolled it up in a strip of rag and tied it tight. It was a sort of pull, yank, spit and tie sequence, each lock the same, and lulled me into tranquil submission with dreams of soon-to-be achieved glamour.

Grandmother had "naturally curly hair" and never quite understood how I had managed to emerge from the womb looking like an awkward, gangly doll the Maker had left incomplete. It must have added to her dedication to the task of putting me up in rags in order to correct this obvious mistake on the part of the Almighty.

When she was done, she gave me a little shove and a loving pat and said, "There now. Run off to bed." Whatever discomfort I felt from sleeping on the knots wasn't noticeable as I dreamed of emerging in the morning a vision of respectability in my curly hair. Putting up my hair went on through the years always with no visible or lasting results. But Grandmother was determined, I was hopeful and my visions of ravishing beauty kept me in a state of willing submission.

Whenever we got ready to leave for any occasion, we were dressed and "washed off" with a washrag wrung out from a pan of hot, soft rain water from the cistern. Then Mother finished up all the missed spots at the last minute with spit. Before going out the door, where Father waited with the team and wagon, Mother lined all five of us up and, beginning at our tops, she spit on stray locks of hair to hold them down in some acceptable fashion, removed any remaining remnants of breakfast egg and stray crumbs from faces and clothing, straightened wrinkles, reinforced pleats, gave our shoes a final shine and plastered down any bits of scuffed leather that showed too much. Her ministrations were speedy and effective for spit was at hand, quick and plentiful and could be positioned exactly where it was needed. Taken altogether and everything considered, spit was probably every bit as free from pollution as the rain water from the deep, dirty cistern.

Besides being instantly available and in a seemingly endless supply, spit was easy to carry along on trips. Our only lake for swimming and fishing was a six-mile walk away across the fields. It was reedy and muddy—great for fishing but a hazard to people. As we scurried back and forth, "hurts" were a common occurrence which we doctored with spit. But its real worth was in treating insect bites.

We could spit on a sting to take away the itch or, if physique and dexterity permitted, get the spot into our mouths to suck out the poison. Injuries never bothered us much. If someone yelled, "Ouch!" somebody else advised, "Spit on it," and our fun went on.

Whenever we left for the lake, the river or one of our favorite swamps, Mother tried hard to make sure we were well-prepared to treat life-threatening emergencies. She was particularly concerned about snake bites and charged us, "Cut an X across the two punctures made by the fangs, suck out the poison and *spit it out!*"

She always came down hard on the "Spit it out!" as though she wasn't quite sure if the poison would sicken us or not if we swallowed it.

When it could be a long walk for help, it was just as well that we were supplied with plenty of information, had a sharp hunting knife stuck in our boots and knew how to use it to get rid of poison. As usual, Mother made sure we knew what to do and trusted us to go ahead and do it.

Things being what they were, it was inevitable that spit would become the all-purpose moistener for our household chores. Very early, I learned to spit on my finger to test the heat on the bottom of a sadiron. Like the echo in the cistern, the sound was my guide. If the spit only sizzled, the iron was not hot enough. If it made a snarling hiss, "Sszzitt," it was just right. A quick "pop" when the spit hit meant it was too hot. And I never burned my fingers.

Mother used spit for dampening stubborn wrinkles when she ironed. Starched shirt collars and fronts got her special attention. Sometimes watching her standing there in the hot kitchen beside the stove in easy reach of the heating sadirons, I wondered that she didn't run out of spit.

Mother's ironing made a little tune with a "Sszzitt, sszzitt," to test the iron, a "Scrub, scrub," of the iron on the shirt and every now and then a "spit, spit" on a wrinkle, with the "Clump, clump" of her shoes beating a cadence as she walked back and forth between the stove and the ironing board.

It was another of the comforting sounds that made me feel secure. I knew our clothes would be clean and wrinkle-free and we could "get ready" for any occasion. For five kids and three adults, Mother needed a lot of strength and patience. And a lot of spit.

Spit was handy to tie knots in threads, hold folds of cloth in place, for threading needles and cleaning off lint and dust. A little spit on a rag cleaned a baby's soiled bottom when diapers had to be changed. Spit made dull pencils write when we had no pencil sharpeners and erased unwanted lines when we had no erasers. It stuck paper cutouts to windows and soaked flyspecks off.

Spit was entertaining and educational. We did a lot of experimental spitting: spitting the farthest, the highest and with the most accuracy. We climbed high up in the barn and spit to see who could spit the farthest down and hit a target.

Father spit on his hands to get a good grip on axe and saw handles. We copied him and spit on our hands at every opportunity in order to appear grown up. Exceptionally good spitters even achieved a respectable veneration. It was said that Great Grandmother Dorset could spit tobacco juice and kill a fly without ever interrupting the rhythm of her rocking chair.

Spit was never a dirty or disgusting word. It was a part of our living. We outgrew the uses of spit, like we outgrew horses and buggies, outdoor plumbing, and all the rest of the expediencies born of necessity. It may have been our ability to adjust to whatever situation was at hand that helped us adopt "new fangled" innovations until they became our own and commonplace.

But we never have forgotten. I could manage quite nicely with spit if need be. Even get dressed up for the New Year.

HOT SLOPS

Monday, January 11.

Today, as it is frequently said, "Winter has seized us in its icy grip," which is, of course, the nature of winter. A shrieking blizzard shook us up on Sunday. Blizzards sound like swarms of infuriated bees, mad at the whole world as they try to force their way inside through every crack and crevice of windows and doors, mutter and cuss, scream and shout in frustration. The tighter the house, the madder they get.

I sleep well during blizzards, content, snug and smug. The frenzy and threat of a blizzard make me appreciate how safe I am here in this comfortable, cozy place. In spite of the threatening weather, there are hopeful signs of a coming change in the seasons. The sun shines in my windows at a new angle. The house-plants feel it, begin to stir and put out a few tentative new shoots as if reaching to test the possibilities for growing.

Winters on the Old Old Farm were a particular joy and a fright: colder, fiercer and more threatening than now. By comparison, we just do not have winter anymore, only a cold spell between fall and spring. It probably was because we had less clothing, less heat and less adequate equipment for fighting the weather.

Two times a day, early morning and evening, Father had to go outside to battle his way to the barn and the chicken coop carrying feed and water, gathering eggs and making sure a large part of our food supply did not freeze to death before we were ready to butcher and eat it.

The barn seemed as far away as tomorrow and was often invisible in the blowing snow. Some thoughtful progenitor had located it out in the middle of our first field so it would be "away from the house" to keep manure smells, flies and chaff distant from our living space. There was nothing to protect the barn where it sat out in the open on the flat ground making it subject to every blow the weather offered: fierce, hot sun and driving rains of summer, bitter blasts of winter snow and ice.

When Father stood in the kitchen door and announced, "I'm going to the barn now, Lorinda," everybody stopped whatever they were doing to help him get ready. Going to the barn in winter was an event to be carefully contemplated and planned and never to be taken lightly. Often Father would repeat himself and say loud enough for all of us to hear, "I'm going to make a trip to the barn now," seemingly in an effort to secure more help or more attention and sympathy. He deserved it, for winter trips to the barn meant facing the real danger of frostbite, even possibly freezing to death.

Early in the season, he stretched a rope from the back corner of the house to the barn. It didn't matter that most of it would lie on the ground, he could hold on and feel his way along in swirling snow and blinding blizzards. It was his lifeline. He could not have made the trip without it.

Always fearful for his safe return, on which we all depended, we watched in apprehension while he put on the big old army coat (a relic from some relative who had gone to The War), boots and leggings, a stocking cap secured by several mufflers over his head and always a pair of gloves with too-long fingers and a few holes. By the time he was outfitted and before he smothered, Mother handed him a ten-quart pail of "hot slops," a collection of the day's peelings and left over food which had been warming all afternoon on the back of the kitchen range, and a clean milk pail to bring back our day's supply of fresh milk. The slops had a special odor which identified them with the barn. As Father went back and forth each day, he set the pail in straw and chaff and manure, a lot of which stuck to the bottom. In winter when even the well often froze, water for washing slop-pails was unknown, so day by day the straw and chaff and manure stuck to be burned on while the pails sat heating until they smelled pungent and dirty and made you want to hold your breath.

As soon as Father went reeking out the back door, we all settled down by a frosty window to watch him. And we never left it until we saw him coming back following along the rope for security. Then we shouted, "He's coming! He's coming!" and Mother and Grandmother rushed to get supper on.

While we watched, we could hear the empty slop-pail and the milk pail clanking together in the cold air. We knew that the old army coat pockets would be bulging with eggs still warm from the bodies of the chickens and often a chicken to be killed to make biscuits and gravy.

When Father came in the back door, he brought all the smells of winter cold and the barn with him: of sweet hay and straw and warm milk, of dust and chaff and always, the particular, penetrating odor of animals and fresh manure.

We all rushed to greet him, relieved and joyous that our food supply was assured for another day. Father had made the dangerous trip to the barn and returned safely and we could expect he would be able to go again.

For years, Mother told anyone she could get to listen, how "Bert almost froze his face going to the barn" and of how he "got lost on the way back when he let go of the rope." It was a good story and showed how proud she was of Father's ability to stave off the winter and care for his family.

I have always remembered Father's face in the cold. Of how his angular features turned bright red and how his beak of a nose, with a bump on the end, dripped until the wind blew the drip off. Father's face looked frozen as soon as he stepped outside. Maybe he never ever quite got warmed up all winter long.

Every spring, as garden time approached, he emerged from all the winter's striving as a great hero. Now, whenever winter comes to freeze us and restrict our going about, I think of him hanging on his rope struggling through the snowdrifts with his head bent against the wind and his inadequate clothing plastered against his scrawny body. And always, his nose is dripping. That drip has been as much a part of Father as his dependability and the missing finger he lost in the cornsheller when he was young, before he learned the caution age and family cares could bring.

LAMP LIGHTING

Monday, January 18. The only

thing a day like today is good for is procrastination. Dreary, dark and cold, it makes me think of unpleasant things such as "Winter is surely here to stay."

When winter came to the Old Farm on the hill above Hollandsville to deepen the cold and intensify the dark, we waited anxiously for spring when it would be light enough at both ends of the day to accomplish all of our work and play. More concerned with the lengthening of daylight than the arrival of spring, we welcomed cold, clear January "when the days begin to lengthen and the cold begins to strengthen." Then we watched the sun come up on winter mornings as if the Lord had minted it specially for our enjoyment.

Our lives were ordered by the sun: its rising and setting,

its shining and hiding behind clouds. Whatever we did was done only "if there is light enough" or "while there is still light." It was a condition that directed all of our activities. "Before it gets dark" was a hurrying time to get everything finished before the light was gone. Mother used it to urge us, "Hurry up and get the chores done while you can still see."

Early morning and twilight were special times filled with the ritual of "using the light." Daylight was used to its fullest and never taken for granted. And to create light after sunset was a ceremony we all anticipated with a sort of awe. When the dark came down on us, almost unnoticed to interrupt our day, Us Kids gathered around Mother and coaxed her to light the lamp.

"I'll do it as soon as it's dark enough," she said as she hurried through the last of her daytime housework. And we had to wait while the familiar outlines of home blurred in the dusk to become almost invisible.

Mother made lighting the lamp an exquisite ritual. After she had squeezed the last bit of use out of the end of the day, she took it down from the shelf and set it in the middle of the kitchen table to be safe from jostling, curious children and bustling grownups. While Us Kids stood watching in the almost-dark, she lifted and tipped the glass chimney just enough to reach in and touch the wick with a match and cautiously replaced it between its four fragile prongs. She knew exactly how to adjust the wick: just enough to give the best light but not enough to make it smoke. When, at last, the lamp began to glow, it lighted her face with a special reassured shining that told us another day was completed and evening quiet would begin. Then we all trailed along behind her as she carried the lamp to set it on the library table in the living room and everyone gathered around "to see."

Technology finally did creep toward us there on the Old Farm. It couldn't be stopped. After passing safely through the threat of gasoline lamps and squinting beneath their unaccustomed brightness, we "got electricity." The poles were strung by an itinerant crew of experts who came to do the job. They were a noisy bunch of roustabouts with bleached, windblown hair, white-toothed smiles and bulging muscles they displayed with great pride inviting anyone to admire who cared to watch them work. I hung around the front yard sitting on the big flat stone by the edge of the road watching them and dreaming of growing up to a more mature social level until Mother called me in.

"Those men are from away and we don't know anything about them so stay close to the house," she warned me.

Her caution did a lot to rebuild my slipping self-esteem and made me think the men might just possibly have noticed me there on the front stone. I couldn't really see much while staying close to the house so the attractive fellows and their muscles were forgotten and I soon wondered what I had ever seen in them in the first place.

In order to make the streets (roads) more safe, lights were put in front of each house. All of our friends and relatives had always been able to find us on the darkest of nights but it was a particular mark of pride to be able to give out directions and say, "Turn in at the light," or "We live by the second light." We speculated and worried for a time if we would have a street light "in front" or not. But finally, it sure enough hung there swinging over the road throwing down a circle of pale, yellow light making long shadows dance across the front yard and up against the house where it shown through the big pine trees.

Its brave glow seemed to be winking and blinking, enticing and inviting somebody to shoot it and put it out of its misery. It seemed alive. And shooting it out became one of the neighborhood's more sophisticated sports. To add to the temptation, there was a certain scientific inquiry involved. If someone shot it out, would the lights in the house go out?

Inquiry demanded investigation. So one windy night when the light danced like a demon, it was put to rest with a single .22 rifle shot. And the lights stayed on in the house. There was some tremulous discussion about what the punishment might be. Jail for sure for whoever did it. But we knew the town had no jail and were certain a person would have to be caught in the act in order to be convicted. Of course the best marksman around got the credit, along with some questionable admiration, "Whoever put out that swaying light sure must be a good shot." No one ever knew.

Eventually the town repairman replaced the bulb. Its pale light glowed for a while and danced through the trees. Then, on some dark night when the wind sent the miserable circle of yellow light struggling up and down the road and the great shadows hit against the house, the challenge was too much to be ignored and it would be gone. Subsequently, one of the town fathers would get up in council meeting and say, "McNaught's light is out again. It's always out." And they would vote to replace it with yet another challenging bulb. No one ever made much fuss about it. No one ever seemed to care.

Our electric fixtures never attained much elegance. All we could afford was a single drop-bulb to hang from the ceiling of each room. The illumination was about the same as from our oil lamp except that the bulb was elevated overhead and could be swung around with safety. So we turned on the switches in every room and started "swinging the lights." To get the best effect, we ran from room to room giving every bulb a mighty push, hard enough to keep them all revolving at the same time. We had many windows and the effect when we came up the hill on the dark road toward the house (especially when the light was out) was spectacular. It made the whole house look as though it was dancing on top of the hill.

Our place came to be known as The Mad House. Mad it was—happy, hilarious and friendly with the lights swinging merrily and the windows winking a welcome in the soft night.

Although the twilight was gone forever from inside the house, outside, the yard was full of it and it was all the more enjoyable when we went out to stand beneath the pine trees and watch the windows wink and the house sway with the swinging lights.

Light did not belong only to the day any more. Creating it was no longer a cherished ritual. We forgot its gift. After we "got electricity," winter days lost some of their charm. We no longer welcomed the time when they began to lengthen and the cold to strengthen. Cold January days became a time of dreading the weather as we urged them to pass and spring to come.

Now I look at these days as ones of more cold instead of more light while I huddle inside and wait for time to pass. I turn on the lights too early, shut out the coming night and forget that it can be enjoyed.

The "before dark" and "while there is still light enough" times are gone forever and only one kind of light is left. There is "always light enough." I wonder is that is really enough.

DEATH

Tuesday, January 19.

Death has come to our family. Laurane left us in the night. We had expected it since her cancer was diagnosed. Now the waiting and dreading time is over and we feel relief even in this awesome finality.

We can see how wise she and Phil were when they deliberately indulged their grief so many months ago and planned for the time when she would be gone. He and the children are ready to build a life now, confident they are doing what she would want them to. Their grief is not lessened, but tempered with knowledge and love. They are a magnificent family.

While we were getting ready to leave in an early-morning blizzard for the long, frigid drive to the funeral, I was reminded of those old times of getting ready to face the cold and the comfort of hot flannel rags, warm clothing and caring. We went in spite of the weather and the dangers of travel because that is what the family does. The same as in those old days, we took coffee and sandwiches and extra blankets along. Things don't change much. Food and warmth still assuage grief.

There is a compulsiveness about grief. Society urges mourning as a penance for joy and demands evidence that it has been accomplished. So we went to mourn together that our lives may continue in guilt-free serenity after this brief interruption. The cold made us draw close in the graveside tent. We hugged and murmured condolences while the frigid wind whipped through our best dress-up and inadequate clothing. We listened to the prayers and words of comfort and thought of the warmth of home and food.

It was a mercifully short time there in the cold and we

eagerly hurried back to the neighbors' generous meal to warm our bodies and bring our emotions into balance that we might take up living without Laurane. The eating and visiting gave us a time of being together a while longer, of seeing friends and family we probably would not see again until the next one of us goes. We fed our stomachs and our hearts.

Being together helps us face the future troubled times that will surely come. It satisfies and satiates our need and makes us whole again. Our grief, as well as our joy, is collective.

Without the nearness of the family, grief might not be so complete and comforting. Our emotions do not grow in isolation. Sharing enables us to go on until we find joy again. And going on is better. We have spent our sorrow. The weeks of hopeless waiting are done. There is comfort in knowing it is over . . . for Laurane—and for us.

CHARLEY'S BEARSKIN COAT

Wednesday, January 27.   This is a day for good work, for entertaining the family and paying social debts which for many generations has meant the preparation of food. A ritual never to be taken lightly, it is the currency of social debt retirement.

In those old days on the farm above Hollandsville, we filled Uncle Charley up each Sunday and felt sure he was reimbursed for all that he did for us. When he came to dinner, we arranged it to suit him and all of us bent to his program of living.

During the summer, he ate pretty much on his own in

the big house in town. But winter days dragged. He must have felt lonely and in need of company and someone else's cooking. So each winter Sunday morning we could expect Charley. No matter how bad the weather or deep the snow, we knew he would come, though it was a mile walk from the house in town to the farm on the hill and he had to climb up the road facing the north wind all of the way. It was no small accomplishment for a man well past seventy.

The roads were seldom cleared but after a sleigh or a cutter had passed, it was possible to walk in the track. "Walking in the track" was a common way to get around on snowy winter days.

"Watching for Uncle Charley" kept all five of Us Kids well-occupied, out of the way of adults and safe and dry in the house. We all watched and waited, scratching frost off the dining room window to make a peephole, our finger-nails scratching and screeching as we cleared the glass and wriggled and shoved each other aside in order to get a bet-ter view.

The best way to make a peephole was to lick the frost off the glass when no one was looking. It was hard on the tongue but quick and efficient. Efficiency in getting things done almost always depended on lack of adult surveillance. It often seemed as though "doing what we were supposed to" meant doing things in the least effective way.

Every Sunday morning it was the same: scratching, wriggling, licking and squabbling, trying to keep a clear view to "watch Uncle Charley come." At last we had a con-sensus. Everyone screamed, "He's coming! He's coming!" And we watched him, an apparition of a man plodding along through the deep snow, moving like some great, black-furred animal, hunched against the storm in his bearskin coat.

That coat seemed to be a Place. Charlie did not put it

on—he moved into it. It was a very special part of our lives. The only one of its kind for miles around, it was as much a part of Uncle Charley as his fuzzy, scraggly, grey mustache and his soft, buzzy voice.

It must have been made from a monstrous bear, stretching as it did from his ears to his ankles. The fur was long and shaggy and looked as if it had come directly from the bear on to Uncle Charley. A row of heavy, corded loops ran all the way down its front and hitched to big, shiny, wooden, spindle-shaped buttons. When he had them all fastened, Charley could retreat into its black depths and endure any storm that came howling along.

When he came up on the side porch (no one ever used the front in winter), he shook off the snow and came stomping in sniffling and shuffling looking more than a little like the original bear whose skin he wore. His eyeglasses and mustache were white with snow and frost. On the trip up the hill, he could not make the effort to wipe his face so everything dripped from his nose and eyes and froze. I was sure Jack Frost must look exactly like Uncle Charles in winter.

By the time he had shed his bearskin coat and fought his way through five kids whom he adored and on into the dining room, dinner was on the table with the chicken and biscuits and gravy for which he had struggled up the hill through the storm. Father put on his suit coat, sat down at the head of the table and got ready to serve up plates for each of us from the mountains of food in front of him. He did not just "fill and plate," he served with great care and certain panache. All of us, even Uncle Charley, had to wait to start eating until Father had finished.

We each received a particular piece of chicken, determined not so much by taste as by tradition and supply. Uncle Charley always got the breast—all of it. I never knew much about how white meat tasted and developed a fondness for thighs and drumsticks—as did we all. But four leg pieces and five kids presented a problem which had to be solved with more than one chicken, making another breast available which Charley always ate. Mother and Grandmother each "chose" wings and Father, "the part that goes over the fence last," and the neck.

Early afternoon Charley moved back into the depths of the bearskin coat and started the long, snowy trek down the hill to the big lonely house in town. Us Kids took our places at the frosty windows and, with more scratching and licking to make peepholes, watched him until he disappeared over Hill's Hill on the way back to town.

When we lost sight of him we sighed, "There he goes," followed by a unison, "Ma, now can we go out?" We got ready to go "waller" for the rest of the day to come in at dusk, wet and plastered over with snow to be "swept off" by Grandmother and dried out over, in and around the kitchen range.

The house smelled like wet wool and leftover chicken dinner and another winter Sunday passed almost exactly as all the winter Sundays before. In a week it would come again with intermittent school attendance in between when we decided if it was "too bad outside to walk the mile into town to school."

It was a nice comfortable repeating of events that made up our lives. We knew what to expect and were quite sure it would come to pass.

It was security.

February

SUNDOGS AND SUNSETS

Thursday, February 11.

Winter plods on. The days drag their heavy burden of snow along barely able to keep moving toward spring which has retreated in utter defeat, cowed into submission by frigid temperatures. About the only encouraging thing is the return of twilight which has been around all winter but now comes at a time of day when it is possible to enjoy it.

I lie on the couch, look out the deck window, ignore the media news and watch dusk bring evening on. As each day passes, the sky holds the fading daylight to let it linger a while longer. Winter clouds race along ahead of the wind as if looking for a place to hide, a few birds test the air and stop by the feeder for a late afternoon snack. Traffic slows, neighbors turn into the parking lot. Lights go on. The noises of evening and approaching night are soft and inviting. The return of twilight helps me to endure the rest of winter.

Early spring days were a special time for Us Kids. Often Father called to us, "Come out and see the sundog!" We had absolutely no idea what caused sundogs, only regarded them as portentous blazing streaks of gold and red on either side of the sun put there for our special pleasure.

While we watched, Father never failed to remark, "It's going to storm." And we agreed nodding wisely. We were sure he was right. Sundogs told us to get ready for weather.

At the end of day, Father called from the backyard. "Come out and see the sunset." Then we all went out to sit on chunks by the woodpile behind the house to watch the sun go down over the chicken coop roof.

In summer, the night noises came. Insects buzzing, horses stomping in their stalls, the pigs in the Old Shed giving a few last hungry "Snuffle, shruggles" and the chickens soft, whispering chirps as they fluttered up to the roosts. And all around us, the day folding up for the night to wait for another morning. It was a good time and kept us close.

After a summer storm he called, "Come out and see the rainbow." And we all rushed out fearful it might fade. "There's gold at the end," Father pointed out. Mother never failed to add, "It's God's promise of no more rain." Sometimes we discussed the meteorological aspects of rainbow formation. Most often, we dwelt on the gold.

Each day held something worth our attention and Father urged us on. His "Come out and see!" brought us out to see the first robin, the first violets in Woodson's pasture, a newborn calf. Every day held something worth our attention.

When night settled down, he called us, "Come out! There's a ring around the moon." After we watched a while, we went for walks down the lane. It was a mile round trip, took a long time in the dark and gave us a wild, happy, satisfying sense of adventure. At night everything familiar looked threatening, the hills and hummocks and ruts were obscured. We stumbled along and did not chatter, only listened, fearful of the ordinary become strange.

Someone might try to walk the stones and casually announce, "I guess I'll try to walk the stones," as though to make the dark less formidable with a daytime game when we could travel from the barn to the end of our lane and never need to step on the ground. But, at night, it hardly seemed worth it. So we who did not often give up, stepped off and said, "Oops, I missed."

Everyone acted as if taking a nighttime walk was casual and frequent. We all knew it was not. It was a perilous adventure, but we did not want to admit it. So, when the sunset faded and someone suggested, more as a dare than as an invitation, "Let's go for a walk down the lane," nobody declined for nobody wanted to appear afraid.

Our lives were filled with real dangers and we were well-versed in ways to avoid them. We were not afraid because they were known. The night walk down the lane was an adventure into the unknown.

As we moved through our days on the Old Farm, we thrilled at whatever they brought, aware of their splendor . . . and their threats. Father taught us to understand and to enjoy.

MIDNIGHT HEMORRHAGE

Sunday, February 14. All

the past week I have been waiting to die. The fright generated by a Saturday midnight hemorrhage seemed pretty much the end of the road. But a D. and C. to investigate my insides has proved uneventful, surprisingly painless and quite relaxing—except for some violent indigestion. Next time, if there should be one, I shall wear my glasses and read the Postoperative Instructions regarding outpatient care.

Adah promised to sit with me before, during and after the surgery in order to run errands, make decisions and to see me home and resting. She did it in spite of falling on their icy driveway and fracturing her arm the night before. Adah never fails to tend to duty no matter what the cost to herself.

Hospitals like to get an early start. I think they want to catch you before you are fully awake and can realize what is going on. Adah arrived in the cold, blustery dark to pick me up before six-thirty with Bert doing the driving. I had showered more for nerves than removing dirt and was ready. We got there early and I was flopped onto a bed, pre-oped and rolled onto a cart before I could begin to worry.

There must be something about a general anesthetic that makes me ravenously hungry. I woke before noon in the same bed from which I had started with no memory of anything except that I'd had nothing to eat since midnight and had missed my morning coffee. Adah was still sitting at the foot of the bed waiting and smiling encouragement, her arm noticeably more vivid shades of purple and green than when we had arrived. I opened my eyes and chanted, "Coffee, coffee, coffee," in an abbreviated request for I was still groggy. She grinned in sympathy and started for the hall in search of a machine.

"Not yet!" the officiating nurse stopped her and proclaimed, "She'll soon be sick," in a sort of portent of doom.

This opposition wakened me to almost-conscious reality and I repeated loudly and firmly, "Coffee, coffee, coffee."

The nurses huddled in a corner apparently in an attempt to reach a consensus about my coffee and imminent throwing up. Adah waited, still smiling. About the time I had begun to feel more discomfort from hunger than the pangs of pain from surgery, someone made a decision and said, "She's not going to throw up. Give her the coffee."

Adah made several trips down the hall to get coffee for us both. I watched her through my blurry vision as she came back into the room balancing two cups with her one good arm and noticed she was pretty wobbly herself and felt the best thing to do would be to get out of there as soon as we could and get her home. She looked more miserable then I felt.

Bert came to pick us up and, as we left, someone handed me the Postoperative Instructions which I tucked into my purse and forgot. I could think only of food and remembered that Bert and Adah like to eat early and on time because of Adah's diabetes. A good hot meal for the three of us became my main concern.

"If you want to stop at Sachsman's on the way home, I'll treat," I offered. I still was benumbed but did not realize it. The dreaded dilation and curettage was over and I felt all would now be well. I was ready to resume normal living and had almost forgotten any resolutions I ever had about living more abundantly.

We stopped at Sachsman's, settled into our favorite booth and ordered chicken with biscuits and gravy all around. It came hot and savory, smelled like a quick return to normalcy and reminded me of the contentment of Sunday chicken on the Old Farm.

We finished lunch and I felt fine. Shortly thereafter, Bert and Adah left me at home to settle on the couch and begin a restful recovery. However, it wasn't long before the living room began to blur, I got dizzy and was losing ground fast. So, before I lost consciousness, I called for help.

Dan's phone number was the only one I could remember. "Come, Brother. Come!" I choked and passed out.

Sometime in the afternoon Dan came to sit and spend

the night. Neighbor Beulah stopped by to see how I was doing and stayed to fix coffee, which I could not now drink. I floated in and out of consciousness. Conversation was impossible for me but I tried hard to be congenial and entertaining. I lay like one drugged—with chicken and gravy, no less.

Along late in the afternoon, I got a bearing on my surroundings, staggered to my feet and tottered to bed. "I've just got to rest," I explained apologetically as though it were not self-evident.

Not until morning did I retrieve the Postoperative Instructions, get on my glasses and discover that I should have had "bed rest and only liquids for forty-eight hours." It was good news in a way. I was able to surmise the cause of my terrible discomfort and could expect to feel better. It was good, too, that I had not thrown up and was again hungry.

The old remedy, "Fill the patient and wait," still seemed to be effective. All the while I had lain miserable on the couch, it had never occurred to me to call Emergency. Old habits of independence are hard to break.

CANCER

Saturday, March 6.

The prognosis from my D. and C. came abruptly Monday morning when Dr. Smolett called. "Well, dear, you have cancer," he said as dispassionately as though he were giving me the time of day. It is best to be told like that, right on the line, straight to the point. It happened so quickly I could not believe it. Fortunately, the mind has limits of cognizance and nature protects us with the unbelievable. I think, "Why don't they just cut it out and be done with it?" But it seems that is not the way. I shall trip back and forth to the hospital almost daily. And wait and wait.

Each day when I have to go in for something, it is cold and blustery. At seven in the morning, the rooms have not warmed up from the previous night's cooling. Today technicians put me on a cold metal table in a cold room, squirted dye in my veins to color my insides and took a lot of x-rays. I have not heard anything since Dr. Smollet's brief announcement. It is as if they are all saying, "You have cancer, dear. You stand by now and see all the things we can do with it." There is never any information about what is coming. I go to oncology when summoned, do what they request, come home and wait hoping to hear.

It helps to talk to patients who are going through the same routine. I met some today at the hospital. While we waited to be called, we chatted almost as though our condition was commonplace and universal for all women. In a few minutes we became members of a close-knit group and, after a sentence or two, were old friends, each one offering encouragement and sympathy to the others. We joked and laughed, made plans and developed our own prognoses. And when we parted, it was with the hope we would meet again soon.

I do not know what will happen. I have made plans and prepared papers—in case. Things are in fairly good shape. I can go with hardly a ripple left to show where I have been.

I wait for pathology lab reports, put off thoughts of the future and manage to keep an empty mind. When I know more exactly what is wrong, it will be easier. And again, Nature will protect me, for I shall not quite believe anything I am told.

ETERNITY

Tuesday, March 9. There comes a time in life when one has to face facts, get everything out in the open, take a long perceptive look and make some decisions. This is my time for that. While I have not necessarily given up, I am resigned to whatever may come, feel very much at peace and quite happy. Panic is no good and not for me, better to go along day by day without too much hope or too much despair. A little good news once in a while is cause enough for rejoicing.

Now that I have faced cancer, it does not seem so unconquerable. Once I avoided even mentioning the word, refused to read any articles or helpful hints. They are mundane, inappropriate and unprofessional. The only way to treat a cancer is to turn yourself over to an expert.

We shall see what happens. For the time being, it is enough that spring comes, the sun shines, the wind shifts toward the south and when I wake mornings, it is beginning daylight. Life goes on, a counterpoint to the repetition of the changing seasons.

Maybe that is eternity—God's promise of repetition.

In the long-ago time on the Farm, I thought a lot about eternity. It was like The Place between the bottom of my shoes and the sidewalk. You couldn't tell exactly where it was but you knew it had to be there somewhere. Eternity went on and on. It caught you and never let you go. There was no way out. It went both ways—on and on forever before, and forever after. I didn't like it because I could do nothing about it.

One day I ventured to ask Mother. She couldn't explain it either and put the nexus right back on me saying, "Well, you have always been asking, 'Who took care of the little kids before the little kids got to be big kids?' "

Thinking about Adam and Eve gave me little consolation. They had been created big kids in the first place and didn't seem very real to me anyway. They were folks in a story. I wanted to know who killed the hogs, did the milking and made the gardens. It seemed to me that ever since the Garden of Eden, everyone had had to hoe their own row and I wanted to know who had hoed the first one. I was pretty sure everybody came into the world as a little kid, so somewhere with someone the whole business had to get started.

Mother seemed to be proud of my intellectual interest in such an esoteric matter but after reminding me again how ponderous my question was, she went back to her housework.

Eternity was something like the picture of the lady on the baking soda box holding a soda box with a picture of a lady holding a soda box and on and on. Like Eternity, there was no place it could stop—or begin. The picture of the ladies holding their soda boxes kept getting smaller and smaller until they got so small I couldn't squint hard enough to see them anymore.

Once in a while I went out and looked at the sky where it was all blue with no clouds to hide it and said, "Eternity is up there. I can see into it. It goes on and on." Then the old nagging question would come to me again and I wondered where it could ever start.

I supposed God was sitting up there in Eternity always keeping his eye on me as Mother so often said. It gave me some comfort to load it all on God's lap and helped me forget about the pictures of the ladies holding their soda boxes.

It wasn't long, however, until I became more interested in the wonderful distractions offered by the farm than I was in Eternity. Play and work freed my mind and kept me too busy to think a lot. I enjoyed growing up, of becoming at least a bigger kid than I had been. Maturing muscles began to dominate my mind and I found comfort in thinking I could do whatever had to be done to sustain life—even if I was a little kid.

But I avoided looking at the soda box where it sat on the cupboard shelf. Whenever I did, Eternity came back into my head and gave me shivers I could not explain. When the shiver times came, I went out in the yard, looked at the sky and let God take care of it.

It's about like that for me now. I can put the cancer out of my mind, look up at the sky and leave it to God.

ROTTING AND SCREAMING

Monday, March 15. There should be something in my life besides the weather and my physique. Once in a while, in spite of this chronic disease, I have a few stirrings of ambition and make plans other than to die.

It is the old wives' tales that sweep over me and leave me afraid and a coward. I can hear Grandmother Dorset saying, "You can always tell when there is cancer in a house. You can smell it as soon as you walk in the door."

She made it sound odious and evil, dirty and hopeless. Grandmother had a vivid sensory memory of it for in her time, people "lived with cancer." No one went to the hospital. There were few to go to. Cancer was considered incurable and had to be endured at home where patients remained and waited to die while their friends and relatives watched them do it.

Grandmother seemed to enjoy dwelling on her lurid descriptions of cancer patients' suffering while their infected parts rotted away somewhat like leprosy, only smelling worse. She liked to tell about patients who lay screaming with pain, "begging someone to shoot them and free them from their misery."

One of her favorite stories was about the woman with cancer of her female parts who lay with all her parts exposed, rotting and dying and screaming. Grandmother managed to make exposure of the parts sound much worse than the rotting.

There was a lady who lived down by the Park who had an artificial celluloid nose about the color of a chicken gizzard. Grandmother and I frequently met her on the path during our walks to town. Whenever we saw her approaching, Grandmother never missed leaning over to hiss, "Cancer," in my ear. I got so I expected it. We would see the lady coming, walking along behind her nose and I would wait for Grandmother's sibilant pronouncement. I often wondered why she did it and if she was offering me information or repeating a warning to stay away for fear I might catch it.

I liked the lady a lot. She was fascinating to look at and I often tried to prolong our meetings so I could have a longer time to stare at her nose and make mental conjectures about whether she could smell, if she really breathed through it and if she caught a cold, would it run? The lady seemed nice and kind. Her purplish ivory-colored nose was very much a part of her looks. Had it not been for Grandmother, I never would have noticed it or thought cancer could have rotted it away.

Grandmother feared and dreaded cancer for she had known it in those old times, heard the screams and smelled the rotting flesh. She knew its hopelessness and terror. She may have found comfort in telling her stories over and over for they were some of her better yarns and she liked to see her listeners shrivel up as she went into specifics.

"Hush-hushing" makes it seem more dreadful. Facing it perhaps requires more fortitude than I possess. For now, I shall ignore it, forget it and try to dredge up enough faith to carry me along. Courage, I have. Faith in a recovery is hard to come by.

A spring rain with thunder is promised for today. The

wind prowls around the building and whistles through the chinks of my cracked-open windows. Clouds hurry by as though bent on some important errand and a few birds try out the gusty air. I relax and look forward to a snug day here in my cozy place. The hospital has finally arranged my radiology schedule and I can start trying to recover, do some hoping and praying and make a few tentative plans. As Amy says about her blindness, "It isn't so bad."

No one can tell you how to live with blindness or cancer or calamities but when someone says, "It isn't so bad, I did it," it helps. You never know how to do it until you try.

"TAKE OFF YOUR CLOTHES"

Thursday, March 25.   A day off from the radiology machine. It is good because my association with it has not been enjoyable. They call it a linear accelerator which means nothing at all to me except that someone has told me it squirts electrons into my cancer, destroys selected cells (along with some good ones) and makes me nauseous and apprehensive.

To be told, "Remove all your clothes from the waist down, put on a gown and wait until we call you," attacks my modesty and destroys my personality. The gown is too big at the top and too short at the bottom. I look down its bilious green wrinkles past my bony, bare knees and varicose legs to my bare feet stuck incongruously into my black pumps and resolve to bring bedroom slippers to wear the next time I come. I have forgotten how much hose can do to make my old-age legs look modish and seemly.

I try to appear at ease but find it impossible to sit with a magazine on my lap (which seems to have disappeared along with my clothes), read and wait with any aplomb. When the disembodied voice in the ceiling summons me to be "Next!" I start down the hall feeling I am on my way to execution rather than treatment and am being forced to walk the distance in naked humiliation.

I stretch out on the cold metal table, the technician pushes the green gown up around my waist casually remarking, "No one has any modesty in a hospital." He truly seems to be trying to make conversation and somehow manages to help me feel more at ease as he begins making red and blue felt pen marks on my abdomen to indicate the target area. My muscles contract when he starts to measure and mark and I tell him, "I'm so ticklish it may distort your alignment." He grins and we have become almost-friends. I resign myself to the machine and wait, fearfully anticipating the claustrophobia to come.

As soon as everyone clears the area, I am left alone with the accelerator. About the shape and size of a compact car, it creaks and groans and heaves itself up from somewhere beneath me and stops with a jerk overhead. Then it complains some more and descends until it is almost touching my nose. I close my eyes, wondering what holds it up with no visible support and hope whatever it is will not fail. The monster gives out a few hoarse "sizzunks" which sound as though it is grumbling and muttering to itself, moves around and adjusts its position to attack me from another angle. I feel the least it could do is to sound as if it were communicating with me. It is so impersonal, I wonder if it is really treating me or is up there on some electronic errand of its own.

After a few seconds, it seems to decide it may have missed something, pulls up away from my nose and lumbers around to stop beneath the grill on which my exposed rear rests. I remember there are no red and blue marks on my behind and wonder how it knows where to "shoot" me. Then it jerks and jiggles its way back into position as if to wait for the next victim.

I am still alone in the big, cold room. No one comes in to tell me what to do. But from somewhere another disembodied voice proclaims, "That is all. You can go get dressed now." I slide off the table, make an undignified trip back down the hall to retrieve my clothing and my shattered personality and get ready to leave for home to be violently ill for a few hours.

So, I was glad to get news of a day off. "Enjoy your vacation," the too-happy technician said. After a biopsy yesterday to cut out a few more tissue samples, I can use a day off. Now the medical folks will have another meeting to discuss my case and maybe decide to take out my uterus, et al., earlier than they previously planned and I shall be spared any further contact with the unfriendly and impersonal accelerator. It will be good to get rid of whatever is threatening my insides and have this nightmare over. One day, hopefully, I can reminisce and say, "It was not so bad."

IT'S DONE!

Tuesday, April 27.   At last,

I am able to say with confidence, "Cancer has come to me
and left." Surgeons willing to cut and slash wherever
needed, friendly capable, slightly mean nurses and my loving family have seen me through and hopefully I am cured.

The hospital stay is a blurred memory, brightened by
"my loved ones." I never could have managed without their
care and attention. Fleeting scenes come back to me. I remember the kindness of the staff and the luxurious comfort
of the hospital. "Just push the button and ask," the crisp,
starchy nurse said. I did and got pain pills, nausea pills,
sleeping shots, coffee, tea, chicken soup and TV. The room
was big and filled with flowers. Its bathroom gleamed with
creature comforts and I pretty much enjoyed myself.

There were so many loved ones gathered to sit and wait,
surgery must have thought it was an invasion. Finally, Dr.
Smolett gave out the happy news. "We got it! She's beautiful!" He seemed to be dancing for joy, all of his huge craggy,

capable pounds effervescing despite his weight.

Sometime later, all the friends and relatives trooped to my room to pat me awake, hold the spit-pan and cry a little. In the background I could hear the hovering nurse saying, "Let her hold it herself," as she began to force me into activity almost before I could see. We all relaxed and rejoiced while I threw up. It was over. We could settle back and wait for health and a future.

Now it is done, the return to reality is very slow. My mental state is still tenuous. I live day to day, grateful for each dawn and hoping each night to see another. It is good that we live only a moment at a time. I shall never fully realize what the experience has done to me. It is better that way and better forgotten.

The days drift into the old routine of visiting with friends and relatives, of hopes and worries, watching the weather and waiting for the season to change. Spring is sniffing around not quite sure of staying. A few birds try out some pine branches for nesting outside the back bedroom window. The grass greens a bit. The wind is, by turns, rank then soft. I have my old spring urges to garden and clean. But, for now, it is enough to be at home resting and to spend time developing some of my own cancer yarns and embellishing them for future spinning lest they dim from neglect and fade, forgotten in the past. Old yarns, like old family treasures, need, and deserve, plenty of attention and much careful tending.

SMASHED GRAPES

Tuesday, May 11.   Almost

the middle of May. Summer is flying even as it arrives. After the long winter, this late spring hurries into growing to catch up with the season. Every beast and plant rushes along pellmell and, hit or miss, starts reproducing before the cold can settle down again and bring the long somnolence of winter.

Apprehension often drives a wedge between me and the future and keeps me from scheming and planning. I fear to tempt fate by anticipating too much. But the future demands attention and contemplation no matter how uncertain and bleak it may be. It is not enough to be only grateful that I am alive. Life demands more than gratitude.

Stopped by the local garage today to have the air conditioning in the Old Green Chev checked. We will have our annual argument as to whether its cooling system will work for another year. It has given me problems ever since we met. What with early body rust, poor carburetion and air troubles, it is time we bade each other farewell. I hate to give up its spacious comfort to trade it in on a stubby, ungracious, practical model. We have traveled many long comfortable miles in spite of its troubles.

There is nothing lifts spirits like shopping for a new car. Especially, if you forget the price and how you will ever pay for it and dream away. I dreamed away a lot of dollars this morning. Perhaps, if my progress is still good by fall, I may sign away the rest of life's income and prepare to cruise along in grandeur as I grocery-shop and trip about the country, all the while looking for large dent-free parking spaces and avoiding traffic hazards. There is nothing more catastrophic than the first dent in the shining glow of a new car. Already, I dread it.

It may be better to acquire the first dent in order to stop worrying about it. In the case of our family's first and most impressive car, we did not wait—Mother immediately took care of it.

Father got the car from Dunck's garage which later became known as Dicky Dunck's and finally Dick Dunck's. As soon as Mr. Dunck had been christened Richard, it followed as surely as the night the day that he be called Dicky and finally Dick Dunck, a sort of vocal gulp that carried along all through his life. In spite of his strange appellation, he was talented and reliable and became our omnipresent, ever-dependable source of mechanical expertise when all we had known was horse and people power. By selling us the car, Dicky assured us a swift transition into the Age of Transportation. Up to that time, we only went somewhere to get places we needed to be. Now, we were to travel just to go places not necessarily to get places. In order to hold up our heads socially, we had to abandon Old Flory and her buggy that had taken us down the road, into town to visit relatives, to funerals and on picnics. Now, instead of "going down the road," we were to "take to the highway." And the car was to be our means of getting there.

The only problem with the new car—which was very soon to become The Old Ford—was that no one knew how to drive it. Dicky had given Father some rudimentary instruction, just enough for him to get out of the Used Car Lot and over to the big house in town. It was only about three blocks, not far enough for much to happen but not far enough for much practice either.

Getting the car was a family event and as soon as Father drove (managed to get) the car into our sunny back yard, we all gathered around to marvel at its mechanics, sniff its strange, clean gasoline smell and listen to its unbelievable rumbles and rattles. Then we immediately used our new-fangled telephone to call everyone we knew and to quiz them, "Guess what we have got?"

Right away I was crushed when someone asked "What kind?" and I had to reply, "Model T." With no background at all, I knew a used Model T was an inferior car and not to be compared with the neighbor's Model A. Decadent though it may have been, it was Our Car and we all longed to try it out.

To get Old Flory going to pull the buggy, we only had to take a firm grip on the reins, slap them on her wide, willing, gray back, cluck a confident, "giggie yap," and she obediently went forward. Not so with our soon-to-be Old Ford.

It had three pedals on the floor, one to push to go ahead in low or to let back into high gear, one to back up and one to slow down (brake), two little levers on the steering wheel to adjust the spark and the gas, an emergency hand-brake which forced the going-forward pedal part way down and put the car into neutral and a crank outside in the front beneath the radiator which someone had to spin with a mighty twist to start the engine while, at the same time, standing in front of it. It was evident to all of us that Our Car required a lot more adjusting than Old Flory ever had and that a person most likely needed three feet to work all three pedals on the floor.

Mother was to be first. Father adjusted the spark and the gas, made sure the emergency brake was pulled back to hold the engine in neutral, stepped bravely in front of Our New Car, grasped the crank and gave it a powerful twirl. When nothing happened, he dashed around back into the car to adjust the spark and gas some more, cranked some more and got the engine roaring without breaking his arm or being knocked down and run over.

He did not go into a lot of detail with Mother about getting the engine stopped—he didn't know a lot of detail. But he was firm about pulling the emergency brake back to force the clutch pedal part way down and the car into neutral in order to avoid hitting anyone who was standing in front of it and doing the cranking. After adjusting the spark and gas again, he said, "Well, get in Lorinda," as though he was opening the door to a whole new world for her.

Mother got in with the air of having driven cars all her life, confident that with her well-known mental ability, she could immediately master pushing pedals instead of pulling reins and clucking, "Giddie yap," in order to control a mode of transportation.

She settled into the seat, immediately grasped the wheel with the same firm grip she had always used on the reins in case Old Flory should decide to jump, and Father explained, "Now, when you want to go ahead, release the emergency brake and push the clutch pedal down. This gives you a lot of power in low so you can get moving. Then, when you get going, let it up."

He did not mention much about the brakes. Maybe he forgot or thought she would only go a foot or so ahead and not need a lot of information about braking and holding the clutch pedal part way in to get into neutral in order to stop. It might have been in the back of his head that, if Mother did manage to get out to the street, she would only go around the block and we could all yell, "Brakes! The Brakes! Push the brake pedal!" as she came back past and, after a few trips, she would maybe push hard on the brake pedal (without pushing the clutch pedal in halfway) stall the car and manage to stop.

Anyway, Mother pushed the clutch pedal down hard. Our new car grated its gears in a quick satisfying response. Mother gripped the steering wheel more firmly than she had ever held Old Flory's reins and started straight ahead. On her right was our barn. On her left was Gurner's new, strong, lead-pipe grape arbor Mr. Gurner had recently put up so they "would have an arbor that would last." Between them was the grass-grown drive to exit the yard in order to go around the block—if Mother should happen to get that far.

She must have felt if she had a firm enough grip on the steering wheel, the car, just like a frisky horse, would make the choice and choose the drive. The car chose the grape arbor and plunged in with all its sixteen "horses" roaring in a mighty defiance of inertia, pushing ahead not fast but irrevocably at a sure five miles an hour. Mother tried to extricate herself from the constraining mangled pipes and vines and we heard our about-to-become Old Ford roar as she pushed down harder on the clutch pedal and advanced the gas. Then we watched as the Old Ford mounted the last, smashed support and stalled atop piles of vines and green grapes.

Not much was said afterwards. Somehow Gurner's grape arbor was straightened "good enough to do." The grapes still hung and ripened in the warm summer sun.

Mother practiced some more and said to all the relatives at every chance she got, "You know, I am becoming a better driver than Albert."

We went places for fun, and for errands, for grief and joy. Never again would we ever have a car so satisfying as our first Old Ford. And there was always Gurner's slightly askew grape arbor next door to remind us of that glorious day when Father brought the Old Ford home.

"KERSIN" OIL

Monday, May 17. The days
slide along toward summer, pushed ahead by this early season, hot and dry and August-like. A few thunderheads heave themselves up each afternoon, rumble around a while, squeeze out a few drops of moisture and go muttering back toward the horizon where they hunker down to wait for another day. Repetitious weather is dull and kills my hoping because I gear it to the changing season. I look ahead to "as soon as it rains and cools off," "as soon as spring comes," and "as soon as it warms up."

Hoping is the architect of procrastination. It is possible to hope and never do very much—just sit around and loaf in great content and never feel guilty about being lazy.

A complete recovery makes me vulnerable to getting sick again. The mental adjustments necessary for this experience have been as traumatic as the disease. It is only lately I can look forward to being myself. It must be that I luxuriated in self-pity so much that illness and recovery filled my thoughts and left no room for anything else. There has been no need to attend to the business of living, only to the business of staying alive. I am still quite content to be occupied only with planning and no doing.

The deck is cleaned now. These days are good ones for sitting out there for morning coffee and neighborhood-watching. I experience a few pangs of ambition now and look forward to housecleaning. It has a certain religious quality about it. Grandmother Dorset never showed any signs of religiosity. I never knew her to go to church. But keeping things clean and neat was a religion to which she dedicated her whole life. While she scrubbed and straightened and demanded that we wipe our feet before coming inside, she kept proclaiming, "Cleanliness is next to Godliness." Perhaps she was asking God to bear the burden of her fetish. He seemed to support her endeavors and she made it pretty clear that, if we wanted to get next to God, we had better keep our feet clean.

She liked to scrub and straighten and to make a big fuss about it. Cleaning the house put her in a position of command. It gave her power to tell the whole family what they could and could not do. When she had "Rid it up," as she called it, she could force everyone to adjust their behavior so as not to "muss up anything." It made her the boss and she liked it.

Grandmother believed in her homemade soft soap, scalding hot water, scrubbing brooms, kerosene (she called it "ker-sin") oil and lots of noise. Her soft soap would take the paint off the woodwork, all the dirt and stain from the floor and the skin off anywhere it touched you. She believed the stronger and more vile smelling stuff she used and the more noise she made, the cleaner the result. For her everything had to be "put in its place." And she firmly reminded us, "A place for everything and everything in its place." She called in the Almighty to emphasize the need to be neat and tidy by announcing, "Order is Heaven's first law." It was said around the family that "Melie can get up in the middle of the night and find anything." The middle of the night then meant so dark "you couldn't see your hand in front of your face." If you lighted a lamp in order to find things, the dark lurked in all the corners, crept up to the lamp and pushed its glow into a faint yellow ball which revealed little except how dark the rest of the room was. Mostly folks just went without and waited for daylight to come. Not Melie, she never waited for anything, she went and got it—day or night.

Grandmother could even make the W.C. shining clean. I never knew that W.C. meant water closet and thought everyone called it "double-you-see" in a dignified voice to avoid saying "privy." When I finally found out, water closet did seem pretty ridiculous. The only water it ever received came when rain leaked through its holey roof. The old outhouse presented her with a vigorous challenge to which she rose in glory. Regularly, she stomped her way out there loaded with her pail of hot suds and her scrubbing broom.

First she swept down the walls with the broom ridding it of moths and spiders and webs full of struggling flies. Then she scrubbed the floor and the "holes" with her hot, soft soap suds. When she really wanted to do a good, thorough job, she used lye made from wood ashes and rain water. And last, she sprinkled plenty of lime down the holes. She kept a sack of it in a corner where it would stay dry and we were all supposed to dump a can of lime down the hole every time we "went out." She made going out a real joy and the old W.C. a lovely place to sit relaxed and contemplative. Her cleanliness next to Godliness kept us clean, healthy and contented.

I imagine Grandmother arrived at the Great Gates carrying buckets of steaming suds and her scrubbing broom ready to begin ridding up the Golden Streets. I am sure she

got there because she expected to. She was the most determined individual I ever knew. She had guts.

In the country stillness there on the farm, we could always tell if Grandmother was busy at housework and what
she was doing. The sounds of her daily chores were the
symphony of our lives. There were ordinary run-of-the-mill
noises that had a daily rhythm from the building of the
morning fire in the kitchen range to the final slam-bang of
the cupboard doors which signaled the finish of the supper
dishes and the end of our day.

"Taking care of the milk" was a particularly tympanic
chore. Each morning and night, Father brought in two
twelve-quart pails full of warm cow-smelling, foamy milk
with bits of straw, manure and general barn dirt floating
around on top of the bubbles. No one ever thought about
washing a cow's udder then. Father just kicked a bunch of
clean straw over any manure that happened to be under the
cow, squatted on his three-legged stool, brushed away bits
of chaff and what not from the teats, laid his head against
the soft flank and squirted away singing Wagner's *Tristan
und Isolde* and sending long, arching, white squirts to the
waiting cats who lapped it in mid-air, while the cow chewed
her cud and now and then kicked him as he kept time to the
music with the squirts hitting against the pail's metallic
sides. *Tristan und Isolde* was about his favorite milking song.
Even the cow seemed to shift around and kick in rhythm.

Milking time was a contented time, peaceful and cozy
there in the barn with little concern for dirt. It was one of
the happiest times of my day when Father let me go out
with him through the gathering evening dark to "pail the
cows." After he carefully hung the oil lantern from the
wooden peg on the wall behind the stalls, he fixed a pile of
clean straw for me to sit on while he did the milking, sang
his songs and we discussed the conundrums posited by life

and living and growing up the only girl with four younger brothers.

When Father brought the foamy milk pails into the house at morning and night, the noisy ritual began. Grandmother was quick to take over. She stretched the cotton flannel strainer across the lip of each pail and lifted it, while keeping the strainer tight, to strain the milk out into shallow milk pans for cooling—on the North Porch, of course. Next, she washed and "snapped" the strainer so the bits of dirt that had been floating around on the bubbles and were now caught in the strainer, would float away into the air. The sound was like a rifle shot. It went along with the starting and ending of day, as much a regular part of our lives as sunrise and sunset.

The cacophony of washing the milk pails came next as she slammed and banged them in the kitchen dry sink while pumping cold water in to rinse out the milk. To be sure I understood the process, she yelled at me over her shoulder above her own din, "Don't ever wash milk away with hot water and soap or you will get a slimy paste that sticks to the inside of the pail and won't ever wash off." She never missed a chance to teach me and never interrupted her work to do it. After a banging cold water rinse under the pump, came hot suds, more dexterous spinning and sloshing and a final scalding with hot water from the teakettle. Then she set the pails shining and clean upside-down on the kitchen cupboard counter to dry.

Grandmother must have had three or four hands to be able to hold the milk pails under the spout while, at the same time, pumping water and spinning them around. Washing and scalding required at least one extra set of heat-proof fingers in order to do all the pouring and sloshing simultaneously. She made everything appear to have to be done "Now." And she was always able to do it.

When milking time was over, breakfast started with fried salt pork done in a great, black, castiron "spider." Just to lift it on to the stove was no mean feat and washing it needed extra hands and strength. For scouring, we had sand and gravel from the backyard bare spots and later, a dishrag resembling a piece of chain mail made of little wire circles hitched together to form a "rag" about eight inches square.

It was easiest to put the spider down on the kitchen table, add a little sand from out back and scrub away. Not Grandmother. Somehow she managed to hold the heavy black pan up elbow high, wield the iron dishrag and scrub like crazy. The result was a din second only to Bull Bastoon's threshing machine whistle. Frequently, she held the pan high and attacked its stuck-on spots with a paring knife. Having to listen to that almost loosened your teeth.

Dirt and disorder were Grandmother's sworn enemies. She "rid the chamber" at least once a week—especially the Twin's room. They were addicted bedtime readers of Tarzan stories and in order to stave off hunger until morning, went to bed with handfuls of cookies and apples. Early in the evening, they snuggled down under the one drop-light bulb that hung over their great, white, iron bed with their supply in hand, let the crumbs fly and pitched the cores underneath the bed. They never turned out the light and we all came to believe they were too scared of Tarzan and his apes to get up to do it. No one minded. They were snug and asleep, scared but well nourished. And Grandmother seemed to look forward to cleaning the "apple chankins" out from under their bed.

While she was ridding the chamber, we could hear her upstairs as she scruffed and swished the broom chasing dust and chankins. Then came a great "crack" when she snapped the crumbs from the sheets and a "whoomp, whoomp" as she pounded the feather bed with the broom handle and beat the pillows to a puffy fluff. After the pounding and fluffing, she left the bed—like the W.C.—a beckoning refuge. The foot-thick feather bed under the clean white sheets was impossible to resist. Just hold your apples and cookies and a good book, make a big leap and land in the middle of the feathers and snuggle down in its cozy depths.

Grandmother put her complete trust in her supply of "kersin" oil as a disinfectant, a quick cure for horse colic and as a furniture polish. She was sure "a little kersin oil in the water" was always a good idea for general cleaning and never failed to "feed the furniture" once a week with it for which she kept an old piece of wool underwear to do the job.

She had a reverence for wood. As though, once severed from the tree and dead, it had to be preserved or it would decay. Time was her enemy and she continually contrived means to best its ravages whether it was preserving the corpse of a beloved and deceased relative, the wood of the furniture, pork on the North Porch or old clothes to be ripped and made over. She fought valiantly against time. Even though she knew she could never win, she managed to give it a mighty push back toward eternity. With her contrivance to salvage us food, warm clothes, shining furniture and respectable funerals with the corpse in good enough condition "to view," she gave us regard for life and taught us the means and necessity for its preservation.

Us Kids must have contributed greatly to Grandmother's happiness and sense of worth as we tracked in snow and dirt, tossed about apple chankins, cookie crumbs and dried up sandwiches. And forgot to put lime down the W.C. holes. Without our steady contribution of clutter, she would have had very little to do.

EVERLASTING IMPROVEMENT

Monday, June 21.

I have been here about a year now—one full of joy and grief and worry. As years go, it has been a benchmark. Some things to tuck away and remember, some things to forget. A year to make me wonder what will happen between now and next June.

This is a time for resolutions: get thinner, stop worrying, never offend, save money, spend only for needed things, keep to a schedule and finish my projects.

There are as many astonishing family yarns developing among us as any in that long ago past—just as juicy, fascinating and revealing. Maybe some day before I am much older, and before I forget, I'll put them down, hopefully with understanding and with love. They need to be remembered for they tell us from whence we came and, perhaps, shed a little light on what we shall be. They tell us, too, that each generation does not change much. We are all about the same—no better or worse. Not really much improved. But then, continuous everlasting improvement is impossible.

About the Author.

Dr. Spross holds degrees in elementary science and mathematics education from Michigan State University. She has worked as a teacher and administrator at local and national levels and has written widely in the field. In addition to articles in professional publications, she originated the pioneering supplementary materials in space-age mathematics: *What's Up There, How Far a Star, From Here Where?* and *The Shapes of Tomorrow*. She also authored a self-help for teachers in arithmetic titled, *Elementary Arithmetic and Learning Aids*.

In the development of these materials, she conducted summer workshops for teachers and authors to design space-oriented mathematics for elementary and secondary levels which, after appropriate testing, were distributed to State Supervisors of Mathematics for use in classrooms.

Dr. Spross received special recognition for her significant contributions in developing this unique series of educational supplements for use in interpreting the educational applications of space research.

A former Director of Elementary Science and Mathematics for the Lansing Schools, she has been a television teacher and has had extensive classroom experience. This is her first production of fiction.

Now retired, she currently resides in Okemos, Michigan, where she pursues interests in writing, painting and gardening. She is a native of Nashville, Michigan.

Wilderness Adventure Books
320 Garden Lane
P. O. Box 968
Fowlerville, Michigan 48836

Please send me: _____ copies of *SUNDOGS AND SUNSETS* at $11.95

TOTAL ORDER $ _____   Enclosed is my ☐ check

—Shipping & Handling—	
1 book	$1.50
2 books	2.00
3 books	2.50
4 or more books	3.00

Charge my: ☐ VISA   ☐ Master Card

Card No. _____   Expires _____

Mr./Mrs./Ms. _____

Street _____

City _____ State/Province _____ ZIP _____

Telephone (_____) _____